Fairy Led

Fairy Led

By

Laura White

First Edition

This is a work of fiction. Names, characters, places, and incidents are either the product of the author's imagination or used fictitiously. Any resemblance to real persons, living or dead, events, or places is entirely coincidental.

ISBN: 979-8-234-04784-7

Published independently by Laura White.

First Edition

Printed in the United States of America

For my girls. I would be nothing without you.

Acknowledgements

Thank you to Dr. Chip Palmer for all his hard work editing Fairy Led and Warning of the Wood.

Thank you, Erin Copeland, for being my second pair of eyes once again.

I would like to thank my amazing family and friends for their love and support. Without you, all this would have never happened.

Thank you. I love you all.

Last, thank you, reader, for giving me a chance.

"There's no point in creating art if you have no intention of putting it out into the world."

—Harley Haslem

This novel contains themes and scenes that some readers may find distressing. Reader discretion is advised.

Content includes:

- Violence and fight scenes
- Death and grief
- Emotional trauma
- Manipulation and abuse of power
- Dark magic and corruption
- Blood and injury
- References to captivity and coercion
- Romantic and intimate themes
- Sensitive mental health topics

These elements are part of the story's fictional world and narrative.

Reader discretion is advised.

Laura White

The Wood Remembers

Contents

Sisters bound.

Worlds collide,

No places to hide,

Paths coincide,

Sisters finally intertwined,

It isn't up to fate,

The final decisions will be made,

Love will never fade

NIX

This is not happening. Never in my life did I think I was a princess. I haven't even been in control of my own destiny. This man has his information mixed up. Wait, not a man—a Fae. A Fae lord at that. The last time I checked, Fiona did not date the Lord of the Fae. Well, not that I really knew anything about her, so it could be true for all I know. Aren't the Fae against humans now? Don't they despise us? So how could this possibly be true?

"This just doesn't make sense. I am not a princess," I stutter. The room has been silent since his shocking announcement, and the Fae present look disgusted.

"I am not sure what you mean, for I do not tell lies. It is not my way. You truly are a princess. Now, away with you. You must want to get cleaned up," Lord Briar replies, waving me off like I am a disgusting fly buzzing around him, not the princess he just proclaimed me to be.

"This way, Mistress," says a woman in her early thirties with brown hair and a sad face. I am immediately reminded of Amanda and of what Brone said. Humans who are here are all slaves.

"Thank you," I say, and she sucks in a breath as if she has been struck.

"Nix, you are now a Princess. Do not thank the help," Lord Briar scolds me, over his shoulder, in front of what must be the entire Fae court.

"Yes, Lord Briar," I say, for lack of a better response.

It is so strange to be corrected just for being kind. Maybe kindness is not found here, just like in Bleaker. Bleaker may be horrible, but it's all I have known in this world. The Fae here do not seem as welcoming as Brone, and that is saying something. The sounds of the feast begin to pick up as I am led away to who knows where by the woman whose name I don't know.

We emerge from the great ballroom into a large antechamber. I gasp as I take in all the beauty that I now behold. There are beautiful marble statues all around the edges of the round room and a breathtaking ceiling mural. It depicts two beautiful female Fae dressed in white fighting leathers standing hand in hand, facing what appears to be an army of Fae. The women are beautifully angelic, almost twins of one another, but one has wings, the other has horns, making me think of Heaven and Hell. A realistic-looking nebula serves as the backdrop for the entire painting. I turn to look at the other beautiful Renaissance-style paintings and statues littering the walls and alcoves of the antechamber. I gawk at the women painted on the ceiling, my mouth open, looking upward one last time, and I almost collide with my guide.

"Careful, Mistress," the woman says.

I straighten myself and follow her down the right hallway of the antechamber. Vines are growing along the hallway walls, startling me. How are they even growing inside with only the firelight from the torches on the walls to light them? Strange magic must keep them so hearty. I quicken my pace to keep up with my guide. No electricity seems to be used here, just as in Bleaker. It is odd and otherworldly. This place has a strange kind of beauty. It is almost too strange to feel welcoming at all, and I inwardly shiver.

We round a corner to the left and pass a massive wooden door with carvings of Fae beings reading books. We walk a few more feet and arrive at a smaller carved door, this one covered in nude female and male Fae beings, making me uncomfortable. The woman stops at the door, opens it, and goes through it, and beckons me to follow her. I am surprised yet again by the large public-style bath, looking like something from Roman times.

"Come this way, Mistress," the woman says as she directs me to a bench that runs along the wall around the whole large rectangular tub, the size of a swimming pool. The water is steaming and crystal clear all the way to the bottom of the tub. There is a short bench that runs around the tub, with staircases cut into either side.

"Come, Mistress, we will undress you so you can bathe," the woman says to me, interrupting my inspection of my surroundings.

"Get undressed here? Just out in the open?" I ask her, slightly embarrassed.

"Yes, there is no modesty here. You must not be so self-conscious. This is the way of these… beings," the woman tells me, reaching out toward me for what I assume are my clothes.

"Ok, what will you do with my old clothes? Also, what do I call you?" I ask her.

"You may call me May if it pleases you, my Mistress. Just give me your garments, they will be destroyed, of course," May says, still waiting for me to undress.

"Ok, May, thank—um, I mean, yes, ok then," I say awkwardly, quickly correcting myself to not thank the woman.

I begin to peel off my filthy fighting leathers. I untie the laces on my pants, pull them down quickly, feeling extremely exposed. Then I peel myself out of my tight leather vest and chest harness meant for my knives, now gone thanks to Brone. It is as if thinking of him summons him from the abyss, or whatever place he comes from. I freeze, just stuck like a deer in headlights, standing here in nothing but my undergarments.

He walks in and starts stripping down like it is totally normal, just to get undressed out in the open. He pulls his large white shirt off, exposing his broad chest. I notice his torso is covered in numerous scars, not meaning to stare at him. He turns his perfectly muscled back towards me, and I notice so many thin white scars, crisscrossing his back, with almost no smooth skin left on him. I freeze when I realize it is from being whipped. Zinn's body has many of the same markings on her back and thighs from the lashings we would receive from Mod or for doing something incorrectly in training.

I am still staring as he slides his travel-worn fighting leathers down, and I realize what I am about to see. I turn around and wait until I hear the splashing of water before I slide out of my remaining clothes and hand them to May. I dare not look at Brone, so I don't lose my nerve to keep walking to the tub. I don't want anyone to think I am weak while I am here, if it is anything like Bleaker. I am bare from head to toe, but I don't want to look awkward covering the top and bottom of my body, so I go with the top half. I cover myself with my arms and walk awkwardly down the steps into the bathing pool.

"Here are the items you should require," May says, laying a tray down by the edge of the pool. Then she continues, "I shall return momentarily with fresh garments for you, Mistress."

"You are leaving me alone?" I squeak, shooting a look in Brone's direction.

"Yes, if it pleases you, Mistress, I must go get clean garments for you," May replies, and disappears out the door, carrying away my filthy clothing.

I find soap on the tray and begin making as many bubbles as I possibly can around my body to block it from Brone's view. I begin scrubbing my body with the luxurious lavender-smelling soap to keep myself occupied. I move to lathering my hair, and I notice Brone looking at me. He has been here for at least ten minutes and has still said nothing to me. Do people not talk to each other here, or just to half-breeds like me?

"Umm, hello, Brone," I say awkwardly, rinsing the suds out of my hair with my hands.

"You seem to have made quite the splash tonight," he says, eying me intensely, and my face burns.

"Well, people have called me a lot of things, and not once was it a princess," I reply, thinking of the name Daniel loved calling me, 'Nix-aphrenia'.

May returns with a clean gown, the same blue as my eyes, carrying the pack I brought from Bleaker. Seeing the pack gives me hope. Maybe they missed my extra knife I hid in it.

"It has fallen to me to be your guard, so you'd better get used to having a shadow, Nix. Watch your back while you are here, little half-breed. Not everything is as it seems," Brone replies, standing suddenly, and I get a look at a lot of things I wasn't prepared for.

"Wait! What do you mean?" I call out, but he is walking away toward the door.

ANA

I let Brone catch Zinn as she falls into a deep sleep. I don't even know if she will still want to know me after she finds out what I am. Well, I guess I don't care as much about Zinn as I do about Nix. I hope that Nix won't hate me forever when I tell her who and what I really am. Brone and I head to the clearing behind the elementary school, where Nix has come so many times before. She never even realized she was right outside the gate to the Fae world. I can't believe she never found it before, given all the research she's done on all things Fae over the years. I guess it really doesn't matter because I have the Fae charm that will transport us all directly to the Great Tree. I recognized it as soon as I saw it dangling from Zinn's neck and took it, along with the Nuummite necklace, from her neck.

Still, my servitude is not up to Lord Stick-Up-His-Butt Briar's standards, but apparently, my family has been rewarded handsomely. I do not know what bargain they made to owe him my life. Why not my brother's? Why did it have to be me? I guess it would have always been me. Another little girl would most likely trust another girl rather than a boy. Especially after that encounter, Nix had with Daniel as a child. No one wanted to get near her, and I am definitely more appealing than my older brother, if I do say so myself.

I don't even really remember my family as it is. I lived with those humans Lord Stick-Up-His-Butt glamoured into thinking that I was their child. He left those poor people shells of their former selves. They were pretty zombified after what he did to them. They cared for me but never showed me the kind of real love a true parent would. I shake off my self-pity and realize Nix is my family now, and I must find a way to make things right with her.

I am not sure what is planned for Nix and Zinn because they are considered an abomination in our world. One or both should be killed according to the law. They could become more powerful than even Lord Stick-Up-His-Butt Briar if they are allowed to come into their shared powers. For so long now, their true powers have been trapped inside those mirrors.

Power was dispersed so strongly that I even felt it here in the human realm. I assume that Nix was gaining her power from her mirror. What is his plan for Nix? I have been wondering, even before she gained her true power from her mirror, why she is so important to Briar. Nix and Zinn have been on his radar as long as I can remember. Even though Nix was here in the human world, he still had me watch her. I will have to wait and see. I will have to watch her back like I always have and always will. This entire situation is insane.

I need to set some things straight with Brone before he tries anything funny on Zinn.

"Hey, meathead!" I call out to him. He is walking in front of me with Zinn's limp body dangling over his shoulder, making me feel uncomfortable. Brone turns and looks at me, then stops.

"Excuse me, what did you just call me?" Brone asks, anger simmering in his eyes.

"I called you a meathead. Are you deaf? Be careful with my friend, or I will kick your ass, and don't think just because I grew up in her world that I don't know how. I most certainly do know how, and I fight well. So no funny business. You hear me?" I challenge him. I am not sure why I feel so protective of Zinn. It must be because I know it is Nix's real body even though it currently houses Zinn.

"Whatever you say. Hurry up, I have somewhere else I am supposed to be," Brone replies, clearly unfazed by my threats, stepping next to me so I can teleport us to the Great Tree.

There, now, my friend's obligation to Zinn is fulfilled. Now to face Nix. I hope I will come out on top. I walk up to Brone, place my hand on his shoulder, and teleport us to the

Great Tree in the Wood. When we arrive, Brone starts to walk away, and I stop him and ask,

"Can you make sure Nix gets her Nuummite necklace and book back?" I am hoping that if she gets them back, they may cheer her up.

"Lord Briar already had the book delivered to her room. You'd best give me that charm, too. Lord Briar will be wanting it back," Brone says, nodding toward the charm I am wearing.

I take the necklace off and hand it to him begrudgingly. He turns and heads inside, and I follow. I make my way through the winding halls of the palace. I head to my quarters and change out of my modern clothes into something befitting my surroundings. I pull on a crystal-encrusted gown that was lying out on my bed. I am guessing this abomination of a dress is supposed to be some reward.

My nerves are making a tight knot in my stomach with the idea of facing Nix. I know she must be here by now. I make my way through the maze of hallways to Nix's door. I am so anxious. I don't know what she will think of me being here. I guess it is now or never.

"Hey, meathead," I say snarkily to Brone, who is now stationed outside of Nix's door. How is he everywhere I turn?

"Ana," he replies with a slight nod of his head.

"I may need you in a second. Stay close. Nix may want to end me when she finds out who I am," I tell Brone, leveling him with my best doe eyes.

"Those eyes may work on some, but not me. If you are doomed to death this night, that is on you. I am here to protect her, not you," Brone says, leveling with a stare.

Building my courage, I knock softly on the door. Nix opens it, and her eyes flare wide with shock.

"Ana?" Nix questions as she sees me stumbling back into the room with apparent shock.

"Yep, in the flesh," I reply, trying to sound casual, even if this isn't a casual situation at all.

"What are you doing here? Why have you come? Have you been captured as well?" Nix asks, sounding distressed, and she pulls me into her room.

"No. I am here by choice. I have things to tell you, and it may be best if you sit down for what I have to say," I tell her, in a serious tone.

"What do you mean by choice? I don't even understand how it is even possible for you to be here," Nix says, with a confused look in her eyes, and she almost falls into the velvet couch.

"I have to tell you who I really am. Please let me get this all out of me, or I may lose my nerve. Here goes nothing. Nix, I have known about you and your situation with Zinn since we first met." Nix is about to interrupt me, so I hold my hand up, stopping her. "Look, I know this is hard to hear, but it is the truth. I was sent away from my family as a child and given to Lord Briar. Once I was brought to the Great Tree, I was prepared to be moved to your world to watch over you. It sounds wild, but I was to report back to Lord Briar if another Fae ever discovered you. Which, obviously, never happened, because we are here now.

You were never to know the truth about who you really are until now. I was told about you and your sister, Zinn, and that you traded places. I never knew whether to believe him until I spent time with you over the years. I do not know how he knew about your situation with Zinn. Don't even ask me. But I need you to know that the day I introduced myself to you was genuine. I wanted to be, and still want to be, your friend, Nix. This whole situation is totally fucked, I know. But here we are. If you have any questions, please ask them. I am an open book. I could never tell you who I was. I am blood oath-bound to silence and couldn't literally tell you, or I would have.

Also, I may have glamoured you twice: once the day we met, then again to get you to read the book I got you for your birthday." I realign my thoughts and ask. "Did you get the necklace back? Lord Briar had them send the book, and I gave Brone your necklace to give to you," I finish quickly. It is like pulling off a Band-Aid. Just get it done in one go. I look to Nix to gauge her reaction, and she is just staring at the floor, looking dumbfounded.

"I am not sure what to think, Ana," Nix says softly, still looking down.

"I am truly sorry, Nix. I really wanted to tell you, but seriously, I literally couldn't," I say once more, hoping it will lessen the blow I have just dealt her.

"So, you couldn't tell me. I understand that. It still doesn't change the fact that I feel utterly betrayed. Were you ever really even my friend?" Nix asks, looking somewhat dejected.

"I was and will always be your friend, Nix, always. I will always choose you. I have, since the day Daniel was kicking sand in your face, the day we officially met, remember?" I ask, trying to pull her sentimental strings.

"Well, if we are both being honest, I need to tell you the truth, too. That wasn't me that day, it was Zinn. Now that you know that, do you still choose me?" Nix says, finally looking up at me.

"Oh, it doesn't matter who that was. I fucking love you like my own sister, Nix! The girl who helps small animals and sings when you think no one is listening and wanted to be on American Idol," I say, full of desperation for her to understand. Even though it was a shock to me, it was really Zinn who made me feel sorry that day. I know Zinn is not why I remained friends with Nix.

"Also, the girl who wanted to be on American Idol and sings isn't me, either. It's Zinn," Nix says, tears starting to form in her eyes.

"Oh, Nix, none of this matters. I know you, I am your friend! Please don't give up on our friendship. I can help you here. Let me try to help you. Use me if you can to navigate this world. I really can help you here. Keep me close, and I can keep you safe," I reply, desperately trying to save this situation.

"How do you even know if you like Zinn or me?" Nix asks, her voice shaking, tears flowing freely now.

"If I were friends with Zinn, I would be with her right now, not you. Zinn is here, you know? She is locked up somewhere in this place. Does that help you see? I would be down there with her, not up here with you. If I wanted to save my friendship with her, I would be there with her," I press and can tell Nix is getting frustrated and more confused.

This isn't what I expected. The doubt in her eyes turns a knife in my heart. There is no anger as I expected, only doubt. Nix is sitting here crying, thinking that I was never her true friend. That I only want Zinn. Is this how it has always been for Nix? Always wondering if people like her for who she is? Do I even really know who Nix is? It doesn't matter, I choose Nix and I always will.

"I choose you—Nix, I always will," I tell her, desperation in my voice.

"How do we know that it is me you choose? The whole reason you are my friend is because of something that actually happened to Zinn. How would we ever really know that we are even friends?" Nix asks, still looking destroyed by this whole situation.

"Is Zinn sweet? No. Is Zinn the reason we met? Well, maybe, but I am friends with you. I spent the last few days with Zinn, and I know I am not friends with her. I am friends with you. Can we start over? Start from scratch? Please, Nix, give me the chance to really be here for you," I desperately plead with her. All the hope deflated from my chest while I waited for Nix to answer. After what seems like an eternity, she finally looks at me with serious eyes and says,

"Ok, we can try. You and Cadmun are all I have. If we do this, you must never lie to me again. Ever."

"Done!" I reply, no questions asked. I don't know if this will be a sustainable friendship after what I have done, but I can promise her this for sure.

"What happened to Cadmun?" Nix asks, worry swimming in her eyes.

"Who?" I ask, not knowing who the hell that is.

"Cadmun, the guy I was with in the Wood when they brought me here. Where is he? Did they hurt him?" Nix asks again, getting visibly nervous.

"I don't know," I reply, and that is the truth. "Sooo… Who is Cadmun? You like him, don't you?" I ask, wagging my eyebrows, trying to be playful.

"He is a friend. A true friend," Nix says, looking one-hundred-percent serious, and I didn't miss the jab she made at me either. A knock comes from the door, and Brone pokes his nosy head in.

"Are you two done here? It is time to go to dinner, Nix," Brone says, stone-faced.

"Do you know what happened to the boy in the Wood?" I ask, trying to be the friend I just claimed to be.

"He was left safe in the Wood as I promised," he replies, and I look at Nix and see worry in her eyes.

I try and try to lighten the mood by saying,

"Lead the way, Sir Brone," sketching a bow in his direction.

He scowls at me. What a joy he is to be around, and I roll my eyes at him. Nix sees it, and I hear her soft laugh, and hope sparks in my heart.

"No, not you, Ana, you are to see to the prisoner," Brone says, looking frustrated that I don't know about this.

"You are to question her. She is in the lower levels. You go now," he points over his shoulder with his thumb. "The princess must not be late," Brone says with obvious impatience in his voice.

A glint of light on the small table catches my eye, and I see Nix's necklace and book sitting on it.

"Nix, wait!" I call out. I snatch the necklace from the table and bring it to her. "Here, don't forget this," I say, holding the necklace out to her. She looks up and beams at me.

"Could you help me put it on?" she asks softly, and I oblige, my hands shaking, knowing this could be a big mistake as the stone begins to glow slightly from within as it makes contact with her skin.

ZINN

When I come to, I am surrounded by darkness and realize I am in some cage. I examine my space and see that I am now in a life-size version of a birdcage, dressed in a plain white floor-length shift. How did I get here? All this time, I never thought this would be my fate, locked up in a strange place when I woke up yesterday. I am definitely not in Hawthorn any longer, or even Bleaker for that matter. I am definitely in my home world based on the style of dress I am wearing, but I do not know where or why I am here. How did I even get here? The last thing I remember is a white fox, then the car crashing.

"I see you are awake," comes a silky voice from the darkness. A beautiful man steps into the light, and I see it right away. He is no man but a Fae from Nix's books. There is no explanation for his otherworldly, breathtaking beauty. Beautifully sculpted features, hair white as snow, eyes like kyanite, and the most telling trait is his pointed ears.

"Who are you?" I ask, scared for the first time in a long time.

"To you, I am Lord Briar, and I am also your father," he tells me, stone-faced, with no emotion behind the statement he just made, making the hairs on the back of my neck perk up.

"You probably have a lot of questions, but alas, I am very busy. I just wanted to see you with my own eyes. I will send someone to talk to you and answer all your questions," he says and turns and leaves me in utterly bone-chilling silence.

I sit here stunned by what I have just been told. My father? How could that even be? A Fae and a Lord at that, whatever that means. Shaking off my astonishment, I realize I need to scan my surroundings. I notice there is a privacy screen at one end of the circular cage. I stand and walk over to it. Looking behind it, I find a privy pot, a water basin, and a pitcher of water sitting on the floor. Well, they thought of everything, I guess.

I look at the cage door and rush over to the gate to see if I can somehow jimmy the lock. As I approach the cage bars, they buzz with what sounds like electricity. I reach for the cage door, and I am rewarded with a sharp and terrible shock. Well, there is some sort of enchantment on this cage, great. I try to pull Wind to me and blast at the door, but it doesn't answer my call. Damn it. My magic must be blocked somehow. I walk the perimeter looking for any weakness in the cage. A door opens at the other end of the cavernous room, shining light into my cage. The light blinds me for a second, and the figure comes into view. I would recognize that red hair anywhere.

"Ana! Help me! Get me out of here. Thank Spirits you are here," I say, relief flooding me as she approaches.

Yet she doesn't rush to my aid but walks slowly towards me in a formal gown covered in iridescent crystals, making her look as if she's covered in fiber optics. She doesn't have a key in her hand. She looks completely alien to me in this moment, and then it dawns on me. How is she even here? Realization hits me that she is somehow part of this, and I am stunned into silence.

"I am not here to set you free, Zinn, but I am here to answer any questions you may have about the current situation you find yourself in," Ana says without a hint of feeling in her voice.

How does she know my true name, and how is she part of this, whatever this is?

"What am I doing here?" I ask, her voice shaking a little, true fear gripping me in a way I have ever known.

"You are now in the Great Tree in the Wood. Lord Briar has found it necessary to lock you here until the time comes to show you to the Fae world," Ana says, like a robot, cold and unfeeling.

"What do you mean when the time comes? Time for what? Why am I here? Who are you really? What is happening, Ana?" I plead with her, hoping she will still help me.

"Lord Briar has had his plan since he found out about your existence when your foolish mother made those mirrors and stole the charm that was around your neck until last night," Ana says, in a cold and unfeeling, sterile way devoid of any of her real personality.

My hand flies to my neck, and I feel the Nuummite and Fairy charm necklaces are no longer around my neck.

"What plan? What is going on?" I question her again.

"It is Lord Briar's plan and not mine, so you should ask him. Now, where is your mirror?" Ana asks, and a smell of rancid milk hits my nose, forcefully making me gag.

"I thought you were my friend," I say, as I almost wretch up my stomach contents, "I always thought of you as my friend. How is this possible? How are you even here, and how do you know who I really am? What is that smell?" I say, feeling like a helpless child falling to my knees.

"What do you mean by smell?" Ana looks at me questioningly.

"It smells awful, make it stop. I think it is coming from you," I say, gasping.

"Well, no glamour, I guess," Ana whispers to herself. "I will have to just spell things out for you. I was brought to your world by Lord Briar to watch over Nix and make sure no other Fae came sniffing around her. I know who you are because Lord Briar told me about you when I first came to Nix's world. I was to watch you both, I guess. But to you, Zinn, I am no friend. I was and always will be Nix's friend ever since I had to stop Daniel fucking asshat from kicking sand in her face because of you," Ana spits, some of the fire I know her to have coming out, but a lingering question in the depths of her eyes.

"Hahaha… Do you really think that was Nix? Do you think she would have sat there without crying? That was me, you dumb backstabbing bitch," I say, laughing and crying at once.

"What are you talking about? That had to be her. You would have attacked the boy," she says, unsure, backing up a step, confusion lighting her eyes.

"Are you kidding me? I have to hold everything in when I go to Nix's world. I have only been myself, my real self, for the last few days, you idiot. Nix would have been in the mental hospital for sure if I didn't put my head down and figure out how to 'play nice'. Or I really would have ruined Nix's life," I throw back at her through my tears.

"Why would you ever want to ruin her life in the first place?" Ana asks, steeling her voice and schooling her features into a fierce, piercing gaze, all the confusion gone.

"Do you think as a small child I knew what I was doing? I looked into a mirror into another world. Do you really think a child would know what they were doing? Do you think I had some nefarious plan when I opened that mirror? Do you think I knew I would end up ruining someone's life? Wow, you really must think I am truly heartless," I say, realizing this is how she sees me. The villain. How could she think I knew what would come from me looking in that mirror? I know Nix thinks I did it on purpose, but I never meant for any of this to happen.

"All this talking is pointless. This is how things are now. You stay here in a cage, and your sister gets to be the next ruler of our world. Now, where is the mirror?" Ana demands again, but her voice is a little shaky this time.

"I will never tell you," I say, not wanting to be helpful to whoever this new version of Ana is.

"They will find a way to make you talk. You know that, don't you?" she says, her voice once again devoid of all emotion.

"Let them try. Do you think pain is something new to me? What do you think was happening to me while Nix was in her world? What messes did I have to clean up for her? The things I had to endure because of her weaknesses? The beatings. The starvation. No, you may think you know me, but you don't. We definitely are not friends if you never thought about what it was like for me to grow up.

Since you knew that I existed this entire time, and I am sure you must be familiar with the people in Bleaker. Why don't you ask the infallible Nix about the life I lead? Ask her who Mod is, and maybe you could understand why her world was so amazing to me. I was a child. Of course, I wouldn't look away from something so good. Leave, I have nothing more to say to you," I tell her my truths, and if she sees fit to make me a villain, then I guess that is what I must be. Still, she seems to flinch a little at my words.

"Fine, but it might not be only me who comes to ask next time, and you'd best believe they will not put up with your disrespect," Ana says with what almost looks like tears.

Then she turns away from me quickly and disappears back through the door she came from, leaving me in darkness once more, making me unsure if I saw her face properly at all.

I scream, then I sob freely, full of turbulent,
unfamiliar emotions that I don't even try to hide because no
one can hear me or see me anyway.

DANIEL

Nix is gone. Ana is gone. They are both just gone. I can't believe they disappeared. I wish I'd had just a little more time with Nix. Authorities still don't know what happened. They are trying to say Ana was drunk and crashed, but none of us drank that night. Also, even if that was the case, why would they both be missing? People have been searching, but there is no trace of them. It is as if they just fell off the face of the earth.

I felt so much for Nix. I wish I had known her better. I don't even have a picture of her to remember her by, except for the one Seth took of her throwing up on the dance floor. It is like my time with her was just a dream. Nothing but memories. I miss her face, those beautiful gray eyes, the ghost of her lips on mine. I fell for her, and it was hard and fast. I don't know what is wrong with me.

All that is left of her is in a small box that I found in my car. It has been a few days, but I am not ready to know what is in it. I thought about taking it to her mom, but there were always so many cops around. I didn't want to get in the way. I feel a strange possessiveness of this box, like it is mine—something to remind me of her for me and me alone. I don't know what is wrong with me.

I feel lost without her. The need to make sure she is ok is eating away at me. But what can I do? I go to the police station every day and check for updates. I have even spent time aiding in the search, but there are no clues as to where they could have gone. I am losing hope that Nix will be found safe. I lie in my bed feeling defeated. I put in my AirPods and play 'Half of Forever' by Henrik, letting the song lull me to sleep.

Maybe I will find her in my dreams.

NIX

I find that each day that passes, I'm discovering I don't really know who I am. I always kept my head down and tried not to stand out so no one would throw me into a hospital. I kept Amanda and Ana happy, and I helped Cadmun when I could. But I realize I may not even have a personality of my own. Zinn was such a big part of my life. I don't understand how to live without her presence, which constantly complicates my life. I take the hand mirror from the dressing table, and I stare at my own reflection. My own blue eyes stare back, and I contemplate who I am. I am not even in my own body. I notice the flowing black hair framing my face, and it makes me wonder, was my life ever really mine?

So far, I've only seen the walls of this room, the bathing chamber, and the ballroom. My only companion is Ana, and Brone is my constant shadow. I'm still not sure how I feel about that situation. Was Ana really my friend? Was she just Zinn's friend? What is it about me that she really liked? I was quiet. I listened to music. I studied. I trained my body in the human world in secret, just trying to blend into the background. Any quirky things about my personality weren't me. It was Zinn. How do I explain to Ana that she may like a person who doesn't exist in me now? Or maybe she hates the person she shouldn't? Still, how would my life have turned out if Zinn had never looked in that mirror when we were just kids? Would I be the way I am now? Would I have been someone else? Because as I look at my reflection, I still see a person I don't know. I almost know Zinn better than I know myself.

Then there is Cadmun. I feel like he may be the only one who ever really saw me. He saw me that day in the shed, and he saw me every time I showed up. He's the only one I really care about. I think he could tell who I was. I hope he's ok. I hope he made it back safely to Bleaker. If he didn't, I'm not sure what I'll do. He just must be ok. They claimed they wouldn't hurt him, but they also just left him to face the Wood alone.

The Wood is a mysterious place, and I am still not sure what lurks within it after seeing all the Fae in court. Anything could be happening to him. He could be lost, captured, or attacked. My mind swirls with all the worst possible scenarios. Then my mind fills with more of the same questions. Would he be able to tell me who I am? Did he truly see me? Will I ever see him again? If he knew my thoughts now, would he still like me? I may never know.

All the feelings I am feeling right now are not good. Everyone thinks of me as the 'good girl,' as the kind girl. The girl who helps hurt animals, the girl who collects antique books, the girl with AirPods in at all times, singing softly. I was really just a girl searching for a way out. I only helped those animals out of guilt. I only helped them because of what Mod made me do to the ones in her world. Does my guilt make it a good action? Because does guilt equate to good? I'm not sure anymore. Most of my life, I thought I was the good girl. Now I'm not so sure. I always felt more like my true self in Zinn's world, where I didn't always have to filter myself. Now, my feelings are a confusing tangle of hurt, rage, and pain—most of all loneliness.

Still, I want revenge, and not just any revenge. I want harsh, cold, exacting revenge for what Zinn did to me. These aren't the thoughts of a sweet, quiet girl. Now that it seems our connection is broken, maybe now I can figure out who I am. My mind is buzzing with too many questions like bees stinging my brain. The anger mingles with my memories of Zinn. My thoughts are overwhelming me to the point of exhaustion.

Zinn got us into this. Zinn, who Ana really loves, the one everyone really loves, the one with the actual personality. Now I can't let go of the anger seeping through every crack of my fractured soul. All-consuming loneliness fills me next. I can't figure out how I fit. I am like a square trying to fit in a round hole. Utterly defeated, I crawl into the large king-size bed with my dress still on and cry into the pillow. I clutch my necklace from Ana. I feel it warm to my touch, as if it is trying to soothe me.

Tomorrow will be better. Lord Briar said he was going to show me a new kind of magic. I hold on to the hope that I can maybe find myself here in this new place.

CADMUN

I have been lost since the rowan berries ran out. I keep walking in circles. I keep ending up in the same spot with the lake smooth as glass. I am so tired of this. I am so frustrated that I kick a rock in front of me, then send it flying on a gust of Wind, accidentally releasing too much energy from my body. Nothing but thoughts of Nix have been circling in my mind. They almost taunt me just as much as this forest does by keeping me moving in a circle. No matter which way I go, I keep being sent back to the place she was taken from.

It has been a few days, and I have been able to stay under the radar. I hide in the trees at night, covering myself with vines for camouflage, which has been working for me so far. I ran out of food yesterday and have been trying to catch the small game in a snare, but so far, nothing. I can keep my waterskin full by pulling water from the ground, but I must find food soon. I am too nervous to try any of the forest's berries or mushrooms. I have not spotted any plants I recognize as edible during my time here.

This backward world is driving me crazy. All I know is that I do not know what kind of beings inhabit this forest. So far, only pixies seem to get close to me, and then they are usually snarling at me like feral cats. Then there was the centaur, that time with Nix. It is so strange not to encounter normal creatures in the forest. It seems the Wood is animal-free. I hear birds in the day, and yet never see them. I hear the rustling of animals in the underbrush but never see them. I don't know how to get any food or where to find Nix.

I need to try something different, and the only thing I can think of is to remove all the charms Nix gave me. I start with the bread in my pocket. I eat the stale bread since it may be the only food I have for who knows how long. Then I remove the rowan berries from my neck, drop them to the ground, and last, I take my socks and turn them right side out. I can't give up. I hope this works. I hope this doesn't make me more lost than I already am.

Immediately after removing all the charms, a pathway appears in front of me. Stepping stones rise from the earth, making a path to the side of the lake. Well, this is new. Apprehension fills me, but this is the only path that lies forward for me to hopefully find Nix. I guess, here goes nothing. I walk the flagstone path, and the forest seems to be alive. I can now see all the birds I have been hearing, and I see little animals scurrying into the underbrush as I move along the path. My fear of starving is receding, and I feel like I am relaxing a little. The animals are not afraid of me at all, though. They are interested in me, but not scared, which strikes me as odd. But my unease about where I am heading is filling me with dread. The path keeps rising from the ground before me, and I follow it.

Even if I am being led to my doom, this may be the only way I can get back to Nix.

ANA

I walk the corridors of the palace trailing after Nix and Lord Stick-Up-His-Butt.

"You know the tale of the twins Aurora and Poe, Dearest One?" Lord Stick-Up-His-Butt asks Nix, and she shakes her head no. "Well, they were the most powerful Fae ever to walk this world. You see, Dearest One, they almost destroyed the realms with their otherworldly power. They could wield such power because they could merge their powers. They were twins. A merging of two beings as strong as they were was catastrophic for us. They lost control and ripped open the portal to the human realm. This allowed those lesser beings to enter our world."

"Aren't I lesser, though?" Nix interrupts. I stumble because if Briar is talking, you don't interrupt, and I wait for him to strike her.

"Would you like to be more?" he asks instead.

"I would like to be more me," Nix replies, and my heart hurts.

"Well, Dearest One, I can show you a way to claim your Fae nature. Would you like that?" he asks, and I get a sick feeling in the pit of my stomach. "You see, Dearest One, my ancestors found a way to stop the twins and seal most of the portals in this realm. They found a new kind of magic, harnessed it, and brought down the twins. Would you like to know what that power was?" he asks, his head turned toward her.

"Yes," Nix replies, and my heart drops.

"The power of draining Spirit is how we stopped the twins and blocked the humans from fully invading our lands. My ancestors kept it secret until one fool Skylark told a human woman how to wield that power. This led his father, Thorne, to curse the very land in order to poison humans who chose to wield any magic. If they drain Spirit, it corrupts them even more than using elemental magic. But you see, since you are half Fae, it will not pollute you as it does the lesser humans, and it will make you more Fae. Would you like that, Dearest One? To be more Fae?"

Nix turns to Briar and answers, "Yes."

"Then come, let me show you how to become more," Lord Briar says and leads us out to the courtyard, where May, the servant, is waiting, looking around nervously. "Ah, there you are, May. Now, Nix, we are going to start slowly. May will be assisting us, of her own free will. Isn't that right, May?"

"Yes, My Lord," May says and drops into a curtsey.

"Ok, Nix, let us begin," Briar instructs.

"Wait, you want me to drain her Spirit?" Nix questions, the fear obvious in her voice.

"Yes, Dearest One, this will make you more like your people. More like me, and as I said, May has volunteered for this honor," Briar says, and I feel like I may puke. I am not sure I can watch what is about to happen.

Nix shoots a look at me over her shoulder, and I almost shake my head no, but Briar cuts me in half with a sharp look. He raises his hand subtly so Nix can't see. Points it in my direction, and I feel a small amount of Spirit leave my body. My knees go weak, and I lock eyes with him, and he curtly shakes his head for me not to say anything to Nix. So, I dutifully smile toward Nix, knowing there is no going back from here.

"Ok, I do want to know where I fit. I will try this for you, my Lord," Nix says, searching for approval in his face.

"Raise your hand toward May. Let me show you," he says and takes Nix's arm and extends it toward May, facing Nix's palm toward May's chest. "Now, just as you pull from the elements, I want you to reach out to May with your mind, and you will feel it just under the surface, her Spirit. It will feel warm and welcoming. Once you have a hold of that warmth, pull it into you."

"Oh, I have done this before. I did it to get my powers out of my mirror. I think I can do this," Nix says in a confident voice that puts me on edge.

"Yes, it will be just like that. I only want you to take a little. I expect you to control yourself and stop when I tell you to. Do you understand, Dearest One?" Briar says like a parent soothing a small child.

"I understand," Nix replies and focuses on May, and I see that Nix's necklace emanates a soft glow.

Then May's Spirit is being pulled from her body.

"Oh… I feel it," Nix says, and her eyes have a determined look I have never seen before.

"Yes, very good, Dearest One, that will be enough," Briar instructs and lowers Nix's hand.

"I feel it. I understand now. I understand what it is to be more," Nix says, looking in awe at Briar, and I know things will never be the same.

ZINN

It has been a few days now. I am not sure just how many, since I never see the sun. I live by torchlight, and isolation is my only companion. There are no other events besides the meager meals I receive three times a day to let me know that time is passing. I could get used to this, being alone in the semi-darkness, singing to myself in between my meals and morning beatings. It happens every morning, like clockwork, and I am not sure why they keep me alive anymore.

With all this time alone left to my thoughts, I wonder about a lot of things. I wonder what happened to Cadmun. Was he ever really my friend, or does he feel the same as Ana? When you have lived a half-life in two worlds, it is hard to know if you actually have any friends. My whole life is fractured in two, and it is my own doing.

So, I cry and sing to myself. As I sing 'Move Me' by Wet, which reminds me of Daniel. It especially feels ironic, given my situation. The last time I saw him, I sang to him. I will not lead them to you, Daniel. I will never break for your sake. Thank the Spirits, they don't have mind-reading Fae to find out where I hid the box. If they do have Fae like that, I haven't seen one. Ana will be coming in soon, based on the food that was placed in my cage a while ago. Just as I have the thought, light floods in from what I have learned is a hallway, and two figures step into the room.

"Are you ready to tell me where the box is?" Ana asks, stepping up toward my cage, a cold look in her eyes. She was serious when she said she was never a friend to me.

"No, I will never tell you," I say in a fierce voice, not moving from my position on the floor.

Cue the big buff guy with the whip. Then the cage door is opened and then slammed shut. I am tossed to my knees by the force of the Wind. Then it starts. I am lashed at least thirty times in a row. I don't cry out or even show how much it affects me. This body is not used to the abuse like my own was. My back is covered in crisscrossing whip marks by the time it is over. Every day, they add more lashes. I would be dead by now, but my body heals itself at an alarming rate. My wounds heal just in time to receive more lashings the next day, the fresh baby skin making it hurt worse than it should.

"Tell me where the box is," Ana says again, a hint of impatience in her voice.

"No," is all I say, breathlessly.

I will not scream for them. I will not give them the satisfaction of hearing my pain. Just letting them see me this weak makes my blood boil. I tried to fight off the behemoth the first few times with magic, but mine was blocked by the cage somehow, and his isn't. In my weakened state, I still tried to fight, but I barely landed a few blows until the male used magic to restrain me, shoving my body to the floor, holding me in place with vines. I take it. I can take this punishment for years if I must to keep that box out of their hands.

"Since you will not cooperate, we will be trying something new today," Ana says, sounding slightly guilty. A newfound dread fills me at her tone.

"Yes, as it seems you will not cooperate properly, and glamour no longer affects you or your sister, we must increase our efforts." The sound of Lord Briar's voice booms through the space. "I have been showing Nix the benefits of the use of Spirit draining and how useful it really can be. I will leave you to it, Nix. Come to me when you are done," he finishes and sweeps from the room.

"Good morning, sister," Nix says, joining Ana, who looks uncomfortable.

"Rot in hell," I reply from my kneeling position on the floor of my cage.

I can take beatings. Apparently, I would have highly magnified powers here in the Wood. I wish I could reach out and smack my sister with a big gust of Wind. Knock some sense into her. I never meant to do any of this to her on purpose.

Did they say Spirit? They are going to do Spirit magic. I can only see Mod's face, and I cringe inwardly at what is about to come. Fear has my heart hammering.

"Lord Briar has given me permission to drain your Spirit," Nix says, with a serious look in her eyes, "and I will drain it from you like you drained all the joy out of my life."

Nix reaches the edge of my cage, and the huge behemoth leaves my enclosure. I watch as she lifts her hand, palm extended toward me. Then it begins. The pull of the magic drags me to my feet while the Spirit is siphoned out of me. It feels as if my soul is being shredded into a million pieces, causing an intense, almost unbearable pain that lances through me. Nix drains me, and I can feel the light inside me dim. No one said life is easy, but this is worse than just killing me. It feels like there is no light or hope left in the world as my Spirit keeps seeping out of me.

My vision begins to dim.

"No! Nix, not too much!" Ana cries out.

Once Nix almost reaches my limit, she releases me, and I fall to the floor. This is a new kind of torture I have never known, leaving me feeling like an empty shell.

"Oh wow," Nix says, with a drunk look in her eyes.

I lie on the floor, breathless and weaker than I have ever felt in my life. They all leave me, and I don't know how to feel about what Nix just did to me. I feel drained and broken by all of this, so I cry, and I sing. What is happening to Nix? Does she hate me so much that she would kill me? Probably. And I can't help but wonder if this is exactly what I deserve.

NIX

I have been working with Lord Briar to hone my ability to drain Spirit. Lord Briar says I am a "natural." I never thought I would do it. After seeing how Mod and Jameson were soulless beings, I never thought I would ever even try to drain someone's Spirit. I never wanted to be like them, but if this is the path to freeing myself from Zinn, I will do it. A soft knock comes to my door, and I answer it, shocked to find Lord Briar standing in front of me.

"Come, Dearest One. Let us take one more step towards your freedom from your sister," he says, and gestures for me to follow him.

"Do you really think this will help separate me from her? Draining her?" I ask apprehensively.

"I do. Until we have her mirror, this is the only way for you to become stronger. This is the path you must take to your freedom. There is no other way," he tells me.

"Ok, if doing this will free me from her, I can do it," I say, full of hope at the idea of finally being free.

"You do this, and you will be more useful to me than you will ever know," he says, and I feel even more determined to do this right.

We reach Zinn's prison, and we walk in, and I feel hope at the idea of this working. Brone is still in Zinn's cage, and Ana is questioning her about the box. Lord Briar steps up and announces,

"Since you will not cooperate, we will be trying something new today," Ana says, and turns to look at me, something I can't place in her eyes.

"Yes, as it seems you will not cooperate properly and glamour no longer affects you or your sister, we must increase our efforts. I have been showing Nix the benefits of Spirit draining and how useful it really is. I will leave you to it, Nix. Come to me when you are done," he finishes, and sweeps from the room.

"Good morning, sister," I say, joining Ana, who is shifting on her feet uncomfortably.

"Rot in hell," Zinn shouts.

"Lord Briar has given me permission to drain your Spirit, and I will drain it from you like you drained all the joy out of my life," I say, ready to take my path to freedom.

I raise my hand and begin. I am filled with a rush of energy I have never felt before. Zinn's Spirit almost wants to flood me on its own. As the Spirit fills the cracks of my soul,

I pull and pull. Ana shouts at me to stop, and I reluctantly lower my hand and say,

"Oh, wow," I say, before I can stop myself. I am so full of power like never before, and I feel a sense of justice at the thought of what this has done to Zinn. I turn, leaving her breathless on the floor of her cage, and I go to find Lord Briar. Ana follows quickly behind me. We reach the hallway, and Ana stops me, placing a hand on my shoulder.

"Nix! What did it do to you?" Ana asks, looking at me with fear in her eyes.

"Well, I feel more powerful," I say, still dizzy from the magic swirling inside me.

"No, it has changed how you look," Ana says with wide eyes.

"What do you mean?" I say, touching my face, concerned.

"Your ears. They are Fae now," she says, pointing at me.

I reach up to feel my ears—Ana is right, they are now gently pointed on the ends. Lord Briar was right, this will make me more. It has only been a few minutes, and I am more powerful than I have ever been in my life. The power courses through me, filling me with a euphoria I have never known and giving me a newfound purpose. Destroy Zinn as she destroyed me. I will keep draining Zinn until she understands what it is like to have your life taken away from you.

The power is changing me so quickly. Just one time, and I am transforming into a true Fae just as Lord Briar promised. My ears have elongated to beautiful points. I wouldn't have stopped if Ana hadn't told me to, which is an unsettling feeling. Still, I may find my place in court with my new transformation. I look more Fae now. They won't notice my human side as much. Also, I am so full of power that no one will dare cross me now. I am no longer just a half-breed bastard child of Lord Briar. I am Princess Nix in this moment, and now I have no desire to give up my position here to return to the human world. I finally feel like I am in control of my own fate. Full of my newfound confidence, I pull vines from the wall effortlessly and have them twine up my arms to show how easily the elements bend to my will now.

Now I will drain Zinn's power every morning. Then I will make my rounds around the court. Which I despise, but I must do what Lord Briar commands. I sit next to him on a throne, and he tells me how all of this will be mine. I have to sit quietly in the great hall and sip tea while the other Fae stare at me like I am an abomination. All of them shun me and avoid me like the plague—some glance at me with open curiosity, though. I am an oddity to them, but I am also polluted by human blood. The only thing that keeps this from being completely dreadful is Ana.

"I still can't believe that you are here. I am not even sure if I am happy about it," I tell Ana, being completely honest with her.

"I understand if you hate me forever for doing this to you. I wanted to tell you the truth for so long, but Lord Briar bound me. I couldn't break my oath, or he would have killed my family or me. Possibly even enslaved them here. I do hope you know that I am so sorry, and I will do anything to make it up to you," Ana replies with a voice full of apology.

"I am sorry that that happened to your family," I say softly. Ana is my only lifeline, and I can't just throw away our friendship just like that. What kind of person gives up that quickly on the ones they love? I do love her like the sister I wish I had, rather than the one I do have. I could never turn my back on Ana. I could never betray her like, well, like she betrayed me. We can move past this together. "One chance is what I will give. Do you hear me? One more chance—don't betray me again," I tell her solemnly.

"I will take it," Ana replies, hope in her eyes.

"Have you heard anything about what happened to Cadmun? Remember your newly made promise to me. Don't lie," I ask Ana, and hope she has found something out.

"I have no idea. I don't know what happened to that boy you were with, or who he even is," Ana tells me in a tumble of words. "You are better off asking Brone, Lord of Brooding over there." I asked him the first night I got here, but he says the same thing every time," Ana tells me, nodding her head towards the surly Fae that is always around me.

"I can't get a thing out of him either. I have tried repeatedly. He is my bodyguard or something, even though there is no need for me to have one in the first place. I can take care of myself." I tell her, the new power I obtained this morning coursing through my veins.

"Well, let me ask around. I don't think Lord Briar would tell me even if I asked," Ana says, disappointment in her eyes.

"Lord Briar would never tell us anything. You think I don't know that?" I tell her, "He wouldn't give a second thought about a human boy. But what I do know is that he has some plan to use me. He hinted at it this morning. If you know what this endgame is, you owe it to me to tell me. Can't you just glamour him?" Nix asks, looking at me with hope in her eyes.

"I can't do that to him or any other Fae, for that matter. It isn't how it works," Ana replies. "You can do it too, I think. I know Zinn can do it. I saw her do it to an entire room of people before we came here. Zinn and Lord Briar are the only beings besides me that know that she is capable of doing it to that many people at one time, though. We believe you may have been glamoured before because you are half-human. When your true powers came to you from the mirror, you can now do glamour because you are half Fae. So that is probably why you have Meathead always following you around to make sure no one tries to glamour you. I tried to glamour Zinn the first time I questioned her, but it hasn't worked since we came to the Wood.

Lord Briar says he doesn't trust the court not to try it so that Brone may be for show. You are now very powerful because there was a binding spell on you from Fiona's mirror. She probably bound your Fae powers so you wouldn't stand out in Bleaker. But do not let your guard down around these Fae. Every single one of them would use you for their own means to get power," Ana finishes, and the statement makes me feel as if these beings are no different from the power-hungry humans in Bleaker.

"Ana, you may go," comes Lord Briar's voice, cutting into our conversation. I sit up straighter and place my hands neatly on my lap.

"Yes, Lord Briar" Ana says, with a small eye roll.

"You see them? Not one of them could stand against us," Lord Briar muses, looking at the Fae milling around.

"Well, why would they want to?" I ask curiously.

"All Fae and humans alike crave what we don't have. If one has the choice between plain food and cake, we would choose cake, wouldn't we? If one has power and another doesn't, they crave it. It creates beautiful conflict," Lord Briar surmises.

"And you believe conflict to be beautiful?" I ask.

"Yes, Dearest One, life without power or conflict would be rather dull, don't you agree?" Lord Briar asks with a hungry look in his eyes.

"I guess it is," I reply, contemplating my newfound power and the possibility of not only controlling my destiny but the destiny of others.

BRONE

To have to watch this insipid child, an imposter, dressed up, playing a part in a bigger game than she even understands. I will watch and do as I am told, but this will end in catastrophe if they can't keep the little princess under control. The more power she consumes, the more corrupted she will become. Her human blood corrupts the Spirit she has consumed, even if she is half Fae. The evidence is shown in the changes already occurring in her appearance. Even the other Fae are whispering about her dramatic change. I know it is unnerving for all of us. Nix now radiates power that rivals even Lord Briar himself.

There is one part of this game that I wish I didn't have to play, which is the enforcer. That tiny waif of a thing, Zinn, is holding out against all the pain I must inflict upon her daily. I want to clean those wounds and tend to her. A Spirit as vital as hers is something to be admired by all. Her strength and devotion to whoever she is protecting are steadfast. Her determination is something fierce to behold. When I hear her singing voice as we enter the chamber each day, it is as sweet as the smell of the stars-of-the-Wood flowers.

I am scared of the day that Nix will begin to penetrate Zinn's consciousness with her mind. I want to, no, I need to warn Zinn of what is headed her way. I don't want to see her give up. Her tough Spirit reminds me of myself when I was young, when I thought I couldn't be made to do what I didn't want to do. But we all must come to heel, or suffer the wrath of Lord Briar, which can be severe. I myself was tricked into my servitude to him for trusting the wrong woman and I found out just how wrong a bit too late. I made my deal. I gave my life to save her from a life of servitude as a human slave to this court. Then she turned dark and was corrupted by Spirit draining and the need for power like the rest of these pompous Fae around me.

I have to find a way to get a message to Zinn without alerting Lord Briar, Ana, and Nix. This could cost me my life, but it is already forfeit. I no longer can lead the life I wish, bound as I am to Lord Briar, forced to be whatever he wants: enforcer, whipping boy, or Seeker, depending on his mood. I have nothing to lose. Zinn could live another day to fight Lord Briar and her sister. If she plays things right, she may be able to escape her confines and save her sister from Lord Briar's corruption, or leave this place and never return. But then she would have to seal the gate that remains open to Nix's world to truly be safe from the monsters that seek to destroy her, and no one, not even Lord Briar, has the power to do that.

CADMUN

I see him before I can think. A thick vine is wrapping itself around my body. An old Fae—not an old man. He has a crooked nose, long snow-white hair, and pointed ears. I realize I am in trouble. He steps toward me and says,

"What took you so long? You have been crashing around my home for days now, and usually, all you townsfolk always find me right away," the old Fae says, "Are you dense or something? I made the path here very obvious."

"No! I am no fool. I was trying to find my friend who has been taken. Did you take her?!" I say, struggling in my bindings. I am fighting with all my might, and I try to take control of them with my own magic, but the vines do not give way. They hold strong and tight, with no hint of release, no matter how much I move.

"Struggle all you will, young one. My vines will not give you an inch of movement as long as I have a hold on them," the old Fae replies, looking smug.

"Wait, you are the man under the hill? We were told to find you. The man under the hill has answers to all. It was written by a woman named Fiona," I say, remembering the note. My butt immediately becomes reacquainted with the ground as I am freed from the vines.

"What did you say, boy? It was meant to be a girl or maybe two girls who were supposed to come. How did you find out about this? Tell me," the old Fae says, his voice making me dizzy.

"Zinn, well, no, that isn't right. It was Nix who was supposed to be here with me, but someone took her in the night and left no trace except that Nix left a trail of berries, but she must have run out before they stopped moving. Once the berries were gone, there was nothing for me to follow," I tell him, not knowing how he pulled the information from me.

"Why didn't you save her?" he asks impatiently.

"What do you think I am doing, as you said, 'stomping around' here?" I reply, flustered.

"Who are you, boy? Tell me quick!" he says. A sweet scent fills my nose.

"Why should I tell you anything?" I ask flippantly, as the smell gets stronger.

"I am, as the note says, the man who dwells under the hill. I have guided your people safely through the Wood for generations now. Seeing as I am a Fae, I live longer than most," he says, winking at me, "Still, I remember Fiona. She was a special case, that one. So again, who are you, Sonny?" the old Fae asks, as my nostrils fill with the sweet once more.

"I am Cadmun, son of Jameson of Bleaker," I tell him, not wanting to, but the words fall from my lips.

"Well, I guess it is nice to meet you, Sonny," he says and continues with, "This way, or I might burn the stew I am making for dinner."

Then he turns and walks towards a small cottage that I had not seen before. Now that he said the word, dinner, all I can smell is the savory food made up of who knows what, but I will gladly eat it if he offers me some.

"So, tell me how you have come to be here, Sonny," the old Fae asks as he guides me to his cottage.

"I came with Zinn, no, wait, I came with Nix. It was just Zinn's body, but really Nix," I say, casually as you please. I can't seem to stop myself. I want to tell him everything, and I think that is what I am about to do, and then he asks,

"Now, which of the girls were you with?" he questions me, looking confused.

"I was with Nix. We made it to the lake as smooth as glass. She broke the compact mirror that connected her to her sister Zinn before we came to the Wood. We found Fiona's note inside the compact and planned to come find you. We were attacked by what Nix called a Centaur upon our arrival. We didn't know where to go until we found the note in the compact," I reply, continuing to tell the story. I can't stop myself.

"Both girls have survived. Hmm?" the old Fae says more to himself than me, "It must be that Briar has your friend Nix. Only his seekers could have taken her in the night and not left a trace. Also, the Centaur was probably a minion sent to find Nix by Briar. He is the one who controls the beings of this Wood. He likes to think he is Lord over all things. Briar has been expecting Nix for some time now," the old Fae tells me, then continues, "Come in, let us have something to eat and a long talk."

I smell the sweet, savory food and gladly follow him into his small cottage.

"Sit there," he says and points to a decrepit-looking chair by the fire. He bustles around his small kitchen and comes to sit in his own worn-out chair, then passes me a bowl of stew. I take it gladly, then hesitate as I bring the spoon to my mouth.

"Oh, it isn't poisoned. Eat," he says, and I comply for some reason. "You say you were told by a note to come to me? Why was there only one girl?"

"Yes, the note told us to find you, and there was always only one girl. Nix's body is in another realm. So how could they both be here?" I ask, confused.

"I see she dwells in another place. I always wondered what Fiona did with the other girl," he says contemplatively. "Now, why didn't you come straight to me?" he asks quickly.

"Nix and I came to the Wood, but we never saw a path to get here. Then Nix was taken, and I searched the Wood with no luck. I think I couldn't find you because of the precautions Nix and I took before we came to the Wood," the words spill from my mouth between bites of the delicious stew.

"Precautions? What are you talking about?" he asks, leaning toward me.

"Well, Nix said there were ways to protect us from being tricked by what she called Fairies or Fae. We had rowan berry necklaces, salted bread in our pockets, and turned our socks inside out for some reason," I tell him and continue to eat. The old Fae laughs and says,

"I see now why you were stomping around. Your socks kept you from being Fairy-Led. As for the bread and berries, they are useless," he explains, looking amused.

"So, my socks kept me from finding you?" I ask, astonished that Nix was right about at least one thing.

"Why, yes. The path would have appeared as soon as you stepped into the Wood. I do try to make it easy for you young folk entering the Wood," he says, still looking amused.

"We would have been able to find you right away?" I ask, frustrated.

"Of course, did you not just hear what I said?" he asks as if I am dense. "Now on to bigger things. If your friend is with Lord Briar, we must find a way to reach her," he says, turning serious.

"But how? I can't even find a trail to follow to find her," I say, frustrated.

"There are other ways to reach those we wish to see. Have you heard of mind sharing?" he asks with eyes full of knowing.

"The only mind sharing I have known of is between Nix and Zinn," I say, grinding my teeth.

"Well, I have a special draught called Dream of Advaita that will help aid you in reaching your friend. Do you really wish to save her?" he asks, looking at me seriously. "The only catch is you may become stuck in the mind realm."

My heart races, and my palms get sweaty at the idea of becoming trapped, but I need to get to Nix and fast.

"I'll do it. Show me," I say, determined.

"Do you understand that you may be trapped, unable to return to your body?" He asks, warning in his eyes.

"I don't care, let's do it," I reply, full of hope at the prospect of talking to Nix again.

"Then come, let us begin now. If she is with Lord Briar, time is of the essence. There is no telling what he is up to," he says and leads me to a small room full of all manner of what look like potions.

He rifles through the shelves, then extracts a small, beautifully crafted blue crystal bottle from the back of one of the shelves.

"Here you are," he says to the bottle more than to me. "Come. You need to lie down for this."

"Will it hurt?" I ask, getting nervous, thinking about how mithridatism hurt at first.

"Spirits no. It is actually quite nice. Your consciousness separates from your body, making you feel weightless and one with space and time. Yes, quite lovely," he says with a slightly dazed look in his eyes.

"What do you mean? Consciousness leaves my body, I don't understand," I say, baffled.

"You will see. Come lie down," he says, leading me to a small, shabby bed in the corner of his cottage.

I follow his instructions and lie down.

"You must open your mind and think of Nix and only her," he says, and unstoppers the bottle and hands it to me. "Take three drops: one drop to leave yourself, two drops to connect minds, and the third and most important to return to yourself. Now think of her, and if her mind will allow it, you will be able to speak to her."

I take the bottle and let three drops of the bitter liquid slide down my throat. I lie back and think of Nix. Nothing happens. I concentrate as hard as I can, and I am suddenly lost in a sea of color floating weightless. Time has no meaning. Then things narrow to a single point. I hear a voice in the dark. I would know anywhere.

BRONE

Another morning, another interrogation of Zinn. I know what I must do so she can be forewarned.

"Tell me where it is, Zinn," Ana commands.

"No, I won't tell you. I would never say anything to you again if I could. You are so fake. I hope that Nix sees right through your bullshit and sees you for who you really are," Zinn replies, spitting at Ana.

"Fine, have it your way, Brone, your turn," Ana states flatly as she moves out of the range of Zinn's well-aimed spit, and I enter her cage.

I have my small barbed flogger in my hand, ready to mete out the punishment they think this poor girl deserves for loving whoever she is protecting. It is so painfully obvious, it could only be love. I approach her, and she is already on her knees, facing away from me, accepting her fate. Zinn just obediently sits there. No fight left in her. It has been a few days, and she knows there is nothing she can do to stop me. I raise the whip and flick my wrist, and the thongs bite into the fragile skin on her back. As it does, I feel a phantom pain in my own back. I raise my hand again and softly whisper,

"They are going to try to penetrate your mind."

I say it softly, but her head shifted ever so slightly, so I know she has heard me. I continue to strike her even though my body begs me to stop. I reach five, feeling the sting of each strike on my own flesh, and she yells,

"Stop!" I am so shocked that I do, at the same time, feel a flood of relief that I can stop striking her.

"Ana, I will tell you, but you must promise not to hurt anyone," Zinn says. "Amanda gave me the box, then I left in the clearing behind the playground of the elementary school," Zinn says—her breath coming rapidly.

"Liar, just tell the truth, is it—Amanda or Daniel?! Which one has the box?!" Ana demands, glaring at Zinn.

"I won't ever tell you," Zinn replies.

"This is your last chance, or we really will try and pull it out of you. Seekers have looked everywhere at your house, and Daniel's, and they found nothing, so where is it?" Ana demands, her patience obviously growing thin, then she turns and stalks towards the door.

"My turn. Maybe I can get you to talk," Nix says, entering the room. Nix lifts her hand, palm extended toward Zinn, and the true torture begins. I watch as the vital energy slowly seeps from Zinn into Nix, the sight sickening me. I want to shield Zinn with my own body to end her suffering.

The pull she has on me is growing stronger each day. Zinn falls to the ground, gasping as she is released from Nix's hold on her.

"I won't tell any of you," Zinn yells at Nix and Ana's backs, lifting her chin in defiance.

"You must listen, or they will torture you in a way that can make you lose your mind," I say quietly so only Zinn can hear me.

"Why would you care?" she whispers back, her damaged back facing me, the sight breaking something in me.

"I do not take pleasure in the things I have done to you," I say, barely audibly.

Her head whips in my direction, and I can see the fear hidden behind her eyes. Pity fills me for this girl. I want to save her from what is to come, but alas, I do not think that I will be able to intervene any more than I already have. I could be severely punished just for warning her, or even speaking to her, but I find I don't seem to care. This is what Lord Briar commands, and blood bonds don't bend or break. As I walk away, I throw down the whip by the door, disgusted by the sight of it. There is something that draws me to Zinn. She is stirring feelings in me I thought I couldn't even experience any longer.

ANA

Zinn will not budge an inch. I know it is either Daniel or Amanda who has the box. It can't just be in the clearing. Why would she even say that? To get out of her beating? I don't think so. Does she think she loves the person she's protecting? She said she thought she loved Daniel. Is she even capable of love? I wish I could march up to that asshat Daniel and ask him.

I am not allowed to return to the human world. For fear that I will be discovered and that it would be hard to explain why I am no longer missing. Then, I also couldn't explain why I didn't return with Nix. There would be too many questions. Glamouring the whole town would take more power than I have on my own. I would need help. It is time to start training Nix to use her gift of mind penetration. It will only work on Zinn. The only other Fae that I know of that has this power is Lord Briar, and he must use an elixir to do it. He doesn't want to be bothered with all of this 'nonsense,' as he calls it, making the responsibility fall on me. I don't know why he won't just do it himself. But I must do his bidding, even if I find his methods disgusting. My fear for Nix's very soul is hanging in the balance. I know there is nothing I can do to stop her from draining Zinn every morning.

Training must start right away. If my last night's punishment is any indicator, then my time is short. Unlike Zinn, my back hasn't healed from the lashings I received for my inability to pull any information out of Zinn. My back is on fire as I head to the ballroom to find Nix, where she is expected to be each day, sitting on a small throne beside Lord Briar. Like some sort of pet, he has decided to keep.

Lord Briar likes to show off his new oddity of a daughter. We all know there is an endgame here that we're missing. Hopefully, I can figure it out before something really bad happens to Nix. I reach the ballroom and see her on her throne, scowling at the rest of the court. I know the power is corrupting her, but I fear she won't stop taking Zinn's power until she feels vindicated and free from being in her grasp for so long. I worry that Nix will never be over the past, and she will doom Zinn to a life bound to being drained of Spirit until she is just a husk of a person. I need to get that mirror so Nix can stop. Looking at her as I approach, I realize this doesn't seem like the Nix I grew to love. I shake off those thoughts and take my place, standing next to Nix on her throne.

"Nix, I think that we need your help with Zinn. Please help us break through to her mind and find the location of that box. The more Zinn resists, the longer this will take, and Lord Briar does not like to be kept waiting. His perception of time is different from ours because of his long life. But we still need to hurry this along." I tell her in a hushed whisper, hoping she is willing to try something other than draining Zinn's Spirit.

"What exactly do you need me to do?" Nix asks in an equally hushed tone.

"I need you to penetrate Zinn's mind and find the answers we need," I say, the words filling me with dread of what this could do to them both.

"How exactly am I supposed to do that?" Nix asks, a puzzled look on her face. "I never had control over anything that happened. I don't think Zinn did either. We just traded places at random, and we never connected minds. I only ever met with her once on the astral plane."

"Well, don't you have a mind connection to Zinn?" I ask her with hesitation. "You must, since you are twins," I say, the last word barely audible.

"Yes, I am supposed to, according to my book. But I have only ever talked to her in the astral plane, like I said, and I am not even sure how I got there. It seemed like it was all of Zinn's doing. I am willing to try. Just tell me what I need to do." Nix says. Determination in her eyes.

"I need you to start tomorrow. When we leave tonight, I can give you instructions on what to do. Can you try?" I ask, almost wanting her to say no.

"Yes, I can," Nix says, her voice dripping with venom, making me shiver with slight repulsion.

ZINN

Things seem to be going as normal this morning. Today is like every other day in this hell I now find myself in. I can feel my mind beginning to break. Is all of this torture worth it? Is Daniel worth all this? Yes. I can't tell them. I really do not want anything to happen to Daniel. Why did I leave that box in his car? Why are they so obsessed with the fucking mirror anyway? They have us both. Nix becomes stronger every day due to the torture she inflicts on me. She relishes draining my Spirit to its limits.

"They are going to start today. Do not let her penetrate your mind," the big male named Brone whispers in my ear as he pulls me up to a sitting position on the floor of my cage, his hand lingering on my shoulder longer than it should. The feeling of his hand on me sends a strange sensation through my body that I can't name before his hand is gone.

What does that guy mean that they are going to penetrate my mind? The only thing I can think of is that I astral-projected into her dream because of the sleeping draught and maybe the Nuummite necklace. Magic seemed to find us after Nix got the necklace, which she now never takes off. I can't be sure of anything anymore about my magic since I can no longer access it.

"Wakey. Wakey. Sister of mine," Nix's singsong voice rings through the dark chamber, which is totally creepy. She steps closer to my cage, and there is something off with her besides her new appearance. Since she has been siphoning my Spirit, Nix seems different in so many ways. I don't see any hint of the quiet, sweet girl behind her eyes. I am not even sure I would want to trade places with her now that she has changed so much. Would my Spirit become corrupted as well?

"We may be related by blood, but I am not your sister, and I never will be. I used to feel sorry for you and wanted to fix all the damage I caused in your life, but now I know how dark and twisted you are. You don't deserve my pity," I answer, keeping my chin high, preparing for her assault.

"Thank you for telling me all of that. I will make sure this hurts, since you now know you deserve to suffer. Time to practice, dear sister," Nix replies, her eyes full of a promise and a threat, making me shiver.

"Here, Nix," Ana says, showing her to a comfortable armchair that Brone places in front of my cage. He gives me a serious look, and I shiver.

"Why, thank you, Ana," Nix says to Ana as she takes a seat in the chair provided for her. It is so unsettling for Nix to be held so high on the pedestal that Ana has created for her. Ana's blind obedience is sickening. I don't think Ana really knows who Nix is anymore, either.

"Are you ready?" Nix asks sweetly.

"For what?" I say as I sit on the floor of my cage. I haven't even bothered getting up for any of this. What is the point of this? Is she just going to sit there and talk me to death? I hope she is patient. I have no faith that she will do anything to me more agonizing than what she has already done. I could only penetrate her mind when I was asleep. So will it even work while we are awake? Maybe I should be taking this a little more seriously than I am. Still, I have no faith in her figuring this out with how jacked up on extra Spirit she is. Maybe if I can get hold of her mind, I could switch places with her. Hope swells in me. This could be my ticket out of here.

I could make this backfire so hard they won't know what hit them. Hope. Hope blooms in my chest at the thought of being free again. I could maybe even see Daniel again. There must be a way back to the human world. I know there must be some way. I mean, how did Fiona and Ana get there? There must be a secret path or something somewhere. I need to see more of my surroundings. Maybe I can pull this off. I push the fear out of Nix getting to me first, and I breathe deep, close my eyes, and think of Nix. Anger floods me that isn't my own, and I gasp. Maybe we are more connected than I thought. Could these be Nix's emotions? I know I have to push past the anger and focus on my end goal. Getting to her mind first.

"Zinn!" I hear Nix shout, and I am snapped out of my thoughts. I am trying to focus on what she is trying to do, so I ignore her. I am not going to be caught off guard if she slips through and gets into my mind first.

"Are you listening?" Nix says, her voice is becoming irritated.

"No. No, I am not. I am thinking of how to get out of here, actually." I say straight-faced, without any feeling, being completely honest.

"Sure, you are. Now concentrate," Nix commands me, and I do, but not the way she wants me to.

"I don't think I will, but thanks for asking. By the way, where is Cadmun in all of this? Does he know what is happening to you? I must say you are not looking very well, and not human, I guess I should say." I shoot at her, and she flinches slightly at my words.

"Just stop talking and concentrate," Nix demands like a child.

"Ohhhhmmm… Ohhhhmmm…" I say as I close my eyes and sit in a lotus position, antagonizing her.

"This isn't a joke. I will penetrate your mind, and whoever you are trying to protect will not stand a chance of escaping," Nix threatens. All of her sweetness and childlike voice are gone.

"Blah. Blah. Blah. You talk too much. I am going to sleep now. Thanks for stopping by. Enjoy your day of evil doing, or whatever it is you do," I reply, stretching out on the floor, and trying to relax and open my mind. I will cut off her attempts with my own. All I can think of is beating her entering my mind first. It is her mind I want to get into. I concentrate with all I am as I let myself drift into a deep state of meditation. Nix's voice is telling me to concentrate, which is the last thing I hear before I am surrounded by darkness.

"Nix… are you here?" I call into the blackness. I am in the same place I was when I last astral projected, so where is she? I did it! I must have beaten her here. Maybe, just maybe, I can force my way all the way into her mind and make a run for it.

"Nix, where are you?" I call one last time before I get an answer.

"Zinn! This is all your fault. Where is she? Tell me now." Cadmun demands materializing out of the darkness.

"Cadmun?" I question, wondering where the hell I am.

CADMUN

"Zinn! This is all your fault. Where is she? Tell me now!" I demand as Zinn appears out of the darkness, calling Nix's name.

"Cadmun?" Zinn questions.

"Yes, it's me. Where is she? I know you have her," I respond to Zinn, running toward her, ready to fight.

"How are you here? I am trying to find Nix, not you," she says, frustrated.

"Well, I am not looking for you either," I reply. "What have you done with her? Tell me, or I will end you," I say, taking a fighting stance.

"What are you doing? Do you think you can hurt me with magic or fighting here? You are so idiotic sometimes. This is the astral plane, idiot. You can't hurt me here. Plus, I am not so sure you want to save Nix anymore. She has been greatly changed by the magic she gained from her mirror. Nix drains me of Spirit daily to enhance her newfound power. She is developing an addiction, and I don't think you are going to find the same sweet girl you saw a few days ago. I promise, Cadmun Nix is not in her right mind. She is becoming corrupted by the magic here. You may need to save her from herself, not from me," Zinn says, warning and a bit of sadness in her voice.

"You are lying! You have always tried to ruin things for Nix. I know that can't be true. She would never do anything so cruel," I say in disbelief, thinking of how Spirit magic corrupted Jameson.

"I am not lying, Cadmun. The magic has even transformed the way she looks. She looks more like a Fae than a human now. I don't know what it is about this magic, but it is turning Nix dark. She is losing her goodness and is also full of vengeance in her heart. She wants to punish me." Zinn says.

"Why shouldn't she punish you for what you have done? Why should I believe anything that you say?" I question, anger simmering in my bones at the thought of anything bad happening to Nix.

"Fine, don't believe me, but you will see if you ever find her here in the Wood," Zinn says, then continues, "Where are you, and how have you come to be here in this place anyway?"

"I, too, am in the Wood. I am with the man under the hill. He had me take a special elixir and meditate on finding

Nix. Instead, I found you," I reply, disgust filling my tone as I say the word you.

"The man under the hill? Who is that? Are you in a safe place?" Zinn asks, sounding worried.

"Don't pretend to be concerned. I know you only care for yourself. You always have. All you know how to do is take Nix's life and take all the joy out of her," I reply to Zinn, my anger reaching a fever pitch.

"That isn't true. I met with Nix in this dimension and told her I would stay out of the way so you two could break the connection. I still want to help and definitely want to break my connection to who she is now. I would gladly be rid of any lingering connection I have to the thing she is," Zinn says, her words not matching the sadness in her eyes.

"I just can't believe that that is true. You are just lying to get what you want. I know you, Zinn. I know that power is what drives you, not Nix. You will not poison me against her," I reply, knowing in my heart Nix couldn't be so cruel.

"I am telling the truth. " You may not find who you are looking for when you finally find her, Cadmun. Please trust me, I am not lying to you," Zinn says, pleading with me, tears in her eyes.

"Where is she if you aren't trying to stop us from breaking the connection? Tell me where you are," I demand.

"Well, I am in a cage in a dungeon of sorts. That's all I know. Oh, wait, what did they call it? Umm… Oh, the Great Tree. Find Lord Briar, and you will find Nix," Zinn tells me.

"Come back now, Cadmun," the old Fae says into my ear.

My eyes flutter open, and I am now facing the man under the hill. His face is intently focused on mine, and he says,

"Ah, there you are. I knew you could do it," then with concern and curiosity in his voice, he asks, "Did you find her?"

"No, I found her sister Zinn. I must find Nix. Zinn says Nix is apparently being corrupted by Spirit magic. I am not sure whether it is true. I don't trust anything Zinn says. I did find out Nix is with Lord Briar at a place called the Great Tree. Is that a problem?" I say to the old Fae, hoping I can trust him with all this information.

"That will definitely be a problem," he replies, scratching the back of his head.

"Who is Lord Briar? Why should I fear him?" I ask, trying to understand Nix's situation.

"He is the Lord of these Woods. All you see is his domain. I keep away from all that court life. I am content being here, helping you, young folk, survive your week, then sending you back with no memories of your time here. I have done it for generations. Some, alas, I can not save. They are found here, lost and wandering by others of my kind. They are forced into servitude, into doing Briar's bidding. I do try. I used to fight to save them, but more and more of my kind outnumber me. I wield the elements just as well as Briar himself, but I can't be in ten places at once. It is a shame that the girl has ended up in his clutches. She may be too far gone to save now. I am afraid, my boy," the old Fae says, emotion weighing heavily in his eyes.

"If you are so powerful, why don't you fight this Briar?" I ask him, not understanding why he isn't using his power to gain what he wants.

"That does seem like it should be an option, but I am an outcast banished from my home, the Great Tree, and blocked by magic from entering it. I can find home, but it will not open to me, and it is not my place to restore the balance," he says sadly, turning and walking to sit in an old, overstuffed chair.

"What am I to do? How can I help Nix? I can't just do nothing," I plead with him, feeling desperate.

"At this point, young Cadmun, I am not sure there is anything you can do unless you are brave enough to let yourself possibly be captured or even killed by the other Fae lurking in the Wood. They are just waiting to pounce on your kind," he says in a solemn voice.

"I'll do it, just tell me where to go. I will find Nix and save her from this world of yours," I say, determined.

"And where would you go? If you can reach Nix, where would you go—and that is a big if," he questions.

"Well, back to Bleaker, your kind no longer enter there," I say, stating the obvious.

"Hahahaha," the old Fae bursts out laughing as if I had told a joke, "You really think my kind can't enter your world? What an idiot you are, Sonny. Of course, we can enter your world, but we choose not to set foot on your cursed land. So that plan isn't going to work for you, I am sorry to say," the old Fae says, leveling me with a knowing look.

"Then what do you suggest I do?" I shoot back at him, frustrated.

"The only option would be to go to Nix's true world. Then you would have to get her to use her Fae magic to seal the portal that exists between our worlds. That is the only way to keep her safe. Separate her from the Fae completely. But if she truly is being corrupted by Spirit magic, you may not be able to get her to leave that power and this world behind. Even with all her new power, she may not have enough to seal the portal. Not even Lord Briar has that much power," the old Fae explains.

"I know her. Nix wouldn't let herself become corrupted. How do I get to her, and how do we close the portal?" I ask, willing to do anything, even leave this world behind, to save her.

"The way will not be easy. First, you need to make your way to the Great Tree and hope not to be captured by the other Fae lurking in this Wood. If you managed to get there, you would have to find Nix and convince her to go with you. Then find the charm that lets Fae travel between worlds. Without that charm, you would have to make it to the portal that is across the Wood near your world of Bleaker, making it that far in this Wood would be folly. It is almost a three-day journey. There are only two of the charms in all of existence. They were created long ago by two twins who once ruled this entire world. Briar himself guards the charms. Only he can allow others to use them. You would most certainly have to kill him to steal one. His power is so strong that I am not even sure a human could kill him. If and only if you can get the charm, you would have to have Nix use every ounce of her power to seal the portal on her realm's side. That being said, and not knowing how powerful she is, I don't even know if she could do it on her own. So you both could be dragged right back. Now that I have explained the reality of this situation, do you still want to try?" the old Fae questions me, and I am filled with apprehension for the first time at the thought of trying to save Nix.

"I will do it. Will you help me?" I ask urgently.

"I thought you would never ask," he replies with a wink.

ANA

I am watching my best friend disappear before my eyes. This world has changed, Nix, and I don't know how to get her back. Her sweet smile has been replaced with a permanent smirk. She now adorns her arms with vines that writhe on her like living snakes and has her hair half braided, half up into a crown every morning by May. I didn't realize that Lord Stick-Up-His-Butt would have her drain the Spirit out of Zinn when she came here. If anything, I didn't think he would want her to become more powerful than she already was. I still have no idea what his endgame is. I can only stand by and watch her grow more and more corrupt each day. I am not sure how much longer I can allow this to go on. But how do I stop it?

As I stand quietly beside her throne, I notice that her normally rosebud-colored lips have changed to a darker shade of red, her cheekbones are sharper, and her ears look like true Fae ears. Nix was always beautiful, but the girlish look to her face is gone, and she looks like a Photoshopped version of her old self.

The Nix I know must be in there somewhere. It hasn't even been that long. Why is this change happening? Normal Fae take hundreds of years to be affected the same way she has been from draining Spirit. It must be her human side. It must still be tied to the curse, and that is why she is changing so rapidly.

The other Fae still keep their distance and make remarks behind their hands when Lord Stick-Up-His-Butt isn't looking. I wish I knew what they were saying. I didn't grow up here, so I am not well-versed in all the political ways of this world. I wish I had someone to talk to about all of this. But who? I have no friends among these Fae. I am almost as much of an outsider here as Nix is. I miss having my friend. My thoughts turn to Zinn, and I wonder if she was ever really my friend, too.

"What are you thinking about over there?" Nix's voice breaks my train of thought.

"Oh, nothing good, maybe of how Mr. Meathead looks shirtless?" I say, giving her a smirk, and she softly laughs, the sound sparking hope in my chest. It is her laugh, Nix's real laugh.

"How much longer do I have to sit here?" Nix wines, and the hope deflates in my chest. Her behavior has become like that of an entitled child.

"Not too much longer," I reply and restrain the eye roll I want to make at her.

It is the same thing every day now. Question Zinn, then move on to breakfast, followed by training Nix to use her newfound powers with deadly efficiency, then lunch, then we finish the day with her sitting on her throne. She knows the drill by now and that we'll be here until late evening. We watch the revelers every night, and only recently has she been allowed to drink Fae wine. I must say I didn't expect the Fae to be so raunchy. I didn't grow up here, and I never saw what court life was like. They brazenly partake in open acts of PDA, making my skin crawl. Nix has always been shy and quiet, but has become quite the spectacle in her own right. Once she has had a few glasses of wine, she will join the revelers on the dance floor. She can captivate the whole room with her newfound beauty and the power that exudes from her. They look on with hungry eyes like predators ready to pounce.

"Ana, can you get me some wine? I am so bored. What is the point of my sitting here anyway? All they do is stare at me and talk about me in hushed whispers. Lord Briar barely notices me during the evening. I want to dance. I'm not sure what I'm supposed to do in this place other than what we do every morning," Nix says, sighing heavily, toying with the vines on her arms.

"You know you're supposed to sit here and look pretty, not look bored? I'll be right back with your wine. Don't go anywhere," I say and wink at her.

I walk toward the small table set with charcuterie boards, pictures of ale, wine, and other elixirs that only the Fae elite can drink. I'm not sure what the elixirs are for, but if their behavior tells me anything, it adds some spice to the night. I dutifully pour Nix a glass of wine, then pour myself a glass and drink it in one go. Pour myself another full glass, then I head back towards her throne. I can't believe how strong this stuff is. I'm already slightly buzzed just from that one glass. Still, the wine helps break the monotony of the night. I reach her throne and hand Nix her glass.

"Here you go, my Lady," I say with a mock bow, looking up at her and grinning.

"Ana, what would I do without you here to keep me entertained with your silliness?" Nix laughs again in her sweet laugh.

"I live to serve you, my Lady," I say and smile and wink at her.

"Oh, thank… I mean, um," Nix starts to thank me, but realizes her mistake and just takes a sip of her wine. Her correction shows me she thinks of me as the help, and my skin bristles at the thought.

The night's debauchery is in full swing by the time Nix finishes her third glass of wine. She stands and goes to the dance floor, and the crowd parts for her as she enters the center of the room. I set my drink down and go to meet her on the dance floor, as I do every night. Seeing as all the assholes here don't dare come close to her, I know they won't join her under Lord Stick-Up-His-Butt's watchful gaze. I can't let her be out there alone. We dance late into the night, and I can't help but feel like this new normal isn't so bad in this moment.

BRONE

I watch over the princess in the large courtyard, practicing her newfound powers. It is frightening how powerful she is. She shapes and molds vines in intricate topiaries. She adorns her arms with vines that writhe like snakes under her control. Then she moves to pulling Water from the earth and swirling it around her like a whirlpool, before plunging it back into the ground as if it had never been there in the first place. She is so skilled that it truly leaves no trace that it was ever even there. Lord Briar lords over her, watching every move she makes with hungry eyes.

"Very good, Dearest One. Now let us try fire next," Lord Briar prompts, and Nix obliges him with fire bursting from her hands, destroying the beautiful, delicate topiaries she had just created with a small smile on her lips.

The fire coming from her hands is as frightening as the fire in her eyes. I shiver at the thought of what she is doing to Zinn, her sister, of all people. How could one be so cold? Is she really that unfeeling? When she first arrived, I could hear her crying herself to sleep at night. Now it is just this cold, calculating girl before me, wielding the elements as easily as breathing. Talent like this hasn't been seen in many generations. Fear grips me at the thought of what Lord Briar could accomplish with his new protégé.

Lord Briar is always whispering in her ear in the ballroom. I know not what he is saying, but it can't be anything good. Lord Briar's heart is as frozen as an iceberg. He is leading her down the same path toward callousness. His own machinations changed me forever, making me a pawn to do his bidding. I hope that is not the same fate Nix faces. The more I see, the more I know that her path to darkness is almost set in stone.

What is Zinn's purpose in all of this? The thought of her name brings to mind her beautiful gray eyes. Zinn still holds out, refusing to let them get the information they want from her. I wonder what it is like to feel that for someone. To be so totally devoted that nothing will break your will to protect them. I thought I knew love once, but it was not as devoted as this. How would that kind of love do to me? Would I be able to take every kind of torture to protect it? The only answer that comes to mind is yes. I watch Nix show her unholy powers and think I would take them all on to protect the one I love. Yes. I see gray eyes in my mind, and they pull at a loose thread in my heart.

DANIEL

The last week of school passed by me in a blur. I don't remember the week clearly. I was just on autopilot. I barely passed all my finals and had to complete my and Nix's partner project with a different group. It was the hardest class to get through without her presence. I found myself distracted, staring at the back table we used to share. English was also almost impossible to focus on. I found myself stopping at Nix's seat and missing her more than I thought possible. I just started to sit in her seat to feel close to her. I have isolated myself from Seth and Josh because their company isn't something I want to deal with, especially Seth's.

The cops investigated Seth and his possible involvement in the disappearances. He was cleared in the end. Still, his company is no longer appealing after the way he treated Nix the last night she was with me. His unveiled rage pissed me off so much. It was so satisfying to watch her punch him. I can't believe how powerful that punch was. Seth's black eye still marks his face slightly. I wonder why she forgave me but not him for all the years I spent tormenting her. I am filled with regret and shame for my past. How could I have let myself be so cruel? Maybe I let Seth's behavior dictate my own. It is almost as if he had a bigger grudge than I ever really did. He came up with the name 'Nix-aphrenia' when we were little, and it just stuck.

I finally opened the box to find an empty blue bag and a beautiful mirror. I find I hold it every night, tracing the lettering across the top, wondering what this could have meant to her. Once I realized it was just a compact, I didn't think it needed to be turned in to the police. It was put in my car before anything happened anyway. It must have just been a birthday gift she left in my car. I will keep it as my last memory of her. The words *'To bind the halves of my heart. Sisters torn apart. Portal to another world, to mend my broken heart'*, is etched into the cover of the mirror in beautiful script. I have no idea what that could mean. I rub my fingers across the script, my curiosity finally wins tonight, and I open the mirror.

I sit up quickly when I don't see my face reflected in front of me, but I am met with the face of Nix. Her beautiful gray eyes are somehow dulled by what seems to be hopelessness, her long, black hair spilling over her shoulders. I watch, transfixed as she toys with the ends, and I can hear her singing. The sight and sound startle me so much that I drop the mirror, and the glass shatters into a million pieces on the floor.

A rush of warmth I have never felt rips through my body, filling me up to the brim. The warmth morphs into heat that burns. I want it to stop. It is more painful than anything I have ever felt before. The heat keeps pouring into me, changing some part of me I never knew existed. I collapse to the ground and, shaking. The heat subsides, and I catch my breath, trying to understand what just happened. Now it is almost as if Nix is with me, a fullness in my heart that only she ever gave me lives inside my chest now. I get my bearings and scramble over to the mirror to see what damage I caused to Nix's treasure. It is completely ruined. What have I done? As I pick the broken mirror up from the floor, small bundles of black and white hair tumble onto my floor with a small folded note. What the fuck? With shaking hands, I pick up the note and read it.

Dearest Nix,

If you have found this note, your life is in danger. Do not seek out your sister. She will come to you. You must avoid her world at all costs. Avoid any strangers who will come into your life from this point forward. Trust no one. You must find a safe place to hide yourself. Stay away from the Wood at all costs! This is all the advice I can give you. Please stay safe.

Your most loving mother,

Fiona

What the fuck did I just find?

CADMUN

It took a while, but the old Fae finally packed everything we would need to start our journey. Leaving his cottage, he leads me through the woods on paths I have never seen before. So far, he has managed to keep us undetected for the past two days. He has a way with the plants and animals in the Wood. The greenery parts for him, as if it knows exactly where he wants to go. We sleep during the day high up in the trees. The old Fae creates camouflage to conceal us with his otherworldly powers over the elements. He has so much control over the elements that I have never seen the like of it before.

"It is safer to stay hidden in the day," the old Fae says to me from his position on the branch below me.

"Why? Aren't there more predators at night?" I ask him, feeling like the day would provide us with more safety.

"Yes and no," he says with a knowing glint in his eyes.

"What is that supposed to mean?" I ask him, puzzled.

"Hush now, look for the Seekers' approach," he says and holds his finger to his lips in a hushing sign, and points to a trio of large Fae males walking directly below us. The males in the trio are huge, bigger than me by at least a foot. My heart sinks at the thought of being out of my depth with beings this size. They are searching the surrounding area for something, then one says,

"Do you see anyone over there?" A large Fae with red hair bellows at

his comrades.

"Nothing here," replies a blonde Fae, turning to his red-haired comrade.

"No, nothing, I have lost his trail," a black-haired male with horns replies.

My heart sinks as I realize they are looking for us. I cast a glance at the old Fae, and he is intently staring down at the three males. We stay in our hiding spot, silent for fifteen minutes while they search the area below us, casting glances into the trees. I am so sure we will be seen that I silently slide farther back to the trunk of the tree to be more hidden from view. The old Fae breaks his silence and says, in a low voice,

"They are looking for us. I am not sure why, though," he says, a puzzled look on his face.

"Maybe they never stopped looking for me to begin with," I supply as an answer.

"Maybe, but with all the racket you were making, you would have stood out like a sore thumb. They would have found you by the first day. Something must have changed. If they are hunting you, we need to be more careful tonight. We must move with silent feet and not speak so we can make it to the Great Tree with you in one piece," the old Fae says with a half-smile.

"Well, let's hope we make it to the tree tonight," I say, hoping with all my heart the path will be Fae-free as we travel tonight.

"Rest now, Sonny," he says, and a now-familiar sweet scent fills my nose.

It is full dark when the old Fae shakes me awake, holding his finger to his lips, a signal to remain silent. I search the surrounding area, but see no danger. The old Fae spins his hand in complex motions, dissolving our camouflage. He points to himself, then the ground. He gracefully climbs down from the tree, nimbler than he should be. Once his feet hit the ground, he scans the area, looks up at me, and signals for me to come down from my branch. Once I reach the ground, he speaks in the softest whisper,

"Follow me with silent feet," and that sweet scent surrounds me.

I am as light on my feet as I can be as we walk at a hurried pace, pushed by the wind down the path the old Fae creates. He signals for me to stop, and my heart begins to pound out of my chest. He turns to me and points to the closest tree to us and orders,

"Climb! Now!"

I do as he orders, and he follows me and deftly weaves us into a cocoon of tangling vines.

"I knew we would get one today, I felt it in my bones," the black-haired, horned Fae says to his comrades.

"Still, this is just a girl, not the boy we are all supposed to be looking for. Lord Briar wants him for his new pet project," says the redhead.

Nix, they want me because of her. Nerves fill me, and I wonder if I am running toward my doom.

"Well, coming back with her is better than coming back with nothing at all. We will still get some Spirit from this one," says the third Fae with blond hair.

As I watch, I see the blonde has a girl slung over his shoulder, and my heart sinks as I take in the familiar fighting leathers. I lurch slightly forward, but the old Fae's iron grasp stops me.

"Look again," he whispers into my ear, not lifting his grasp.

I look again, and they are a few feet further ahead, and I see it—her hair. The girl's hair is flaming red. My stomach plummets as I realize it's Echo. I don't know the girl well, but I know it is her. In this moment, I want to save her from whatever fate awaits her. I jerk a bit from the old Fae's grasp, but he holds on tighter.

"Think now, Sonny, it is her or Nix you can't save both without showing your hand here," he whispers, eyes burning with truth.

I stare at Echo, and I can't do it. I can't choose her over Nix. I am so ashamed, but the old Fae is right. I lean back against the tree trunk and steel myself against the onslaught of shame I feel at letting this happen. We wait for what seems like an eternity, and the old Fae releases us from our cocoon, and we travel onward to what will probably be my doom.

ZINN

I feel the tingling, the breath, then I am transported. I am in the center of what seems to be a party. Ana's beautiful face is smiling back at me. My head is swimming like I have had too much to drink. I stumble away from Ana and realize what is going on. I have switched places with Nix. This is it. This is my chance. I look around wildly at my surroundings to try to find a way to escape. There, across the room, I see it: a door. I shove through the throng of writhing bodies and make a break for the exit.

"Nix! Hey, Nix, where are you going?" I hear Ana call in a slightly slurred voice.

The crowd parts for me like I am carrying some illness they don't want to catch. I rush as quickly as I can to the door on the far side of the room, as fast as I can in this cumbersome gown and corset I have on. I reach a large antechamber and freeze. I can run down a hallway to the right. I find a door with naked Fae carved into all kinds of provocative poses, a door with Fae tending to animals in a field, and another door with ornately carved figures of Fae reading. I have no idea where to go, but I need to go somewhere fast. Seconds tick by, and I rush towards a door with the reading Fae carved ornately into its surface. I push through the doors and find I am in a large library, and realize I may have just doomed myself.

Run, my mind screams, so that is exactly what I do. I run down the center of the vast library and look to my left and right as I go, trying to spot an exit. I am almost to the end of the rows, and I see it: a doorway! I cut hard to the left. I slam my shoulder into the corner of the solid wood bookshelf, and a loud pop comes from my shoulder. I stumble, but regain my footing and run while my shoulder screams in pain. I am rewarded with a hallway. I take my chances and keep my pace up, pushing myself with Wind. My labored breathing sounds too loud in the silent corridor. I am not coming across any Fae, which is fine by me, but what I am not seeing is the way out.

The hallway ends at a T intersection, and I turn right without a second thought, and I am rewarded with the sight of a large double door. I am almost there. Then a heavy hand clamps down on my hurt shoulder. I suck in a breath through my teeth, whirl around, and strike my attacker with the heel of my palm to their nose.

"Oof," my attacker grunts, then he takes my arm and wrestles it behind my back.

"You!" I am astonished when I realize it is Brone.

"You?" the male says, switching his grasp on my arm and spinning me so he is now holding me tight against his body in what I could only call an embrace.

As our bodies touch, something strange but familiar brushes against my very soul. I know him. Not my attacker, not my punisher, but something I don't recognize. A stifled sob comes out of me, and the male holds me close and smells the top of my head in a way that should repulse me, but it doesn't. I find myself burying my face into his chest and feeling relief I have never felt in my entire life. I know for some reason he will keep me safe. He has been my only lifeline since I first arrived.

"Zinn?" His gravelly voice grinds out.

"Yes," I whisper back, not sure what is going on, and he grabs my chin and forces me to look up at him.

"You did it," he whispers quickly, then says, "This way. Follow me."

I do just that, knowing that I can trust this male completely. I am not sure how or why, but I know he wouldn't betray me in this moment. He guides me through a maze of hallways with expertise, then the hallway splits and veers to the right, and it begins to transform into an earthen tunnel. We are moving quickly and silently, only the sound of my breath and my heart pounding in my ears. Then he abruptly stops and turns towards me.

"Forgive me," he whispers more with his eyes than his mouth. No sooner are the words said than he leans against the wall, pinning me in, and kisses me hard and fast. I am so stunned, but I don't have time to overthink the moment. He releases me, steps aside, and reveals a door.

"Run. Now," that's all he says in his gravelly voice, and turns back and sprints away with Wind pushing him in the direction we came from.

Without hesitation, I do just that. I run. I wrench the door open only to slam so hard into someone that we both tumble to the ground. I right myself quickly, ready to fight the best I can in this gown. I take up my best fighting stance, and so does the person I collided with. The figure's back is to me; something oddly familiar in its movement. As it turns to face me, I see him.

"Cadmun?"

BRONE

No, not now, why now? How could this be happening now? I thought I was done with having feelings. So why now? Why her? I knew there was something about her that was drawing me in. Those gray eyes, that sweet voice, that determined resolve. Finally, after all these long years of my life, I have found someone who has opened my heart. I found her, and I may never even be able to have her.

I head back to the ballroom, knowing I can't slip up. I must keep Zinn safe. I do not know what will happen, but I must hold on to hope that she will find a way to live, a way to survive. I just threw her to the dogs, and I am not sure I can handle it. Every step takes me further and further from her. If I play this right, I will be the one to go after her. She needs to make it for at least the night. Zinn is tough. She is smart. I know she can do it now. I need to handle some damage control with Ana and Lord Briar.

"Well? Did you find her?" Ana asks, eyes wild.

"No, I lost her," I say, which isn't a lie but maybe not the whole truth either.

"Why would Nix take off like that? This doesn't make any sense. It was a normal night like all the others since she has been here. I just don't understand," Ana is pacing back and forth, and I just stand here silently waiting to see what her next move will be. Ana clearly didn't realize that the princesses switched bodies. I would have never thought it possible if I hadn't seen it with my own eyes. Seen Zinn there in her beautiful gray eyes.

"We must search the palace to notify the staff. I will have to tell Lord Stick-Up-His-Butt," Ana says and turns and heads to the front of the ballroom, and I turn and go to the servant levels of the palace, pretending to notify the staff. I push myself as fast as possible with the Wind, thinking there still may be some hope left after all. I run back to the palace exit, and I find a young man arguing with Zinn, and I knock him out cold. Then I mouth the word,

"Run."

CADMUN

The old Fae and I finally reach a tree that is bigger than anything I have ever seen. It seems to have materialized out of thin air. I never saw it in the distance. How could it possibly have been hidden? It must be the Wood, I realize, and I get an uneasy feeling. How could something so big not be seen?

"Now this is where our real problem begins, Sonny," he tells me, looking at the tree.

"What do you mean? We made it, so what is the problem?" I question him.

"I am exiled, so the Great Tree will not open for me," the old Fae says, his eyes sad.

He touches the tree with longing in his eyes. Those eyes hold more secrets I don't have time to figure out.

"So what are we supposed to do?" I ask, frustrated by this new revelation, and kick a rock, sending it flying with the Wind.

"Well, there is nothing to do but wait, I am afraid. We must wait until someone comes out before you go in, because this is where I must leave you. I have done all I can for you, but I can not enter, so it is up to you to find Nix, the charm, and have her seal the portal. If she can even manage it," he says, as if it will be the easiest thing I have ever done.

"How long will we have to wait? Won't you stay to help?" I ask impatiently, knowing Nix is so close, but I can't reach her.

"I can't linger long. I will wait as long as I can," he says, and I feel some of my anxiety recede.

We wait for what seems to be hours. We have decided to ambush anyone who comes out, and I will make a run for it and hope for the best. Impatience wells up in me. I can't help but feel an urgent need to get to Nix. I keep pacing around the tree, waiting for my opportunity to pounce.

"Will you relax? You're making me dizzy from all your pacing about," the old Fae says, giving me a look of annoyance.

"Sorry, I can't seem to stop myself," I reply honestly.

Just as I am turning to sit down, someone comes crashing into me, knocking me to the ground.

"Watch out!" The old Fae cries out, positioning his hands ready to strike with his magic.

I quickly gain my footing and turn to see my foe, and am shocked by what I see.

"Cadmun?" Zinn questions.

"Oh, thank the Spirits, I was on my way to save you. Come, let's go," I say, reaching for Nix, and that is when I see it. Her eyes. Gray, not blue. I realize my mistake and shove Zinn away.

"Come, we must away now, Sonny," the old Fae says hurriedly.

"Yes, let's fucking go," Zinn agrees, starting to make a move towards the Wood at my back.

"No. You tell me now, where is she?" I demand and grab her by the arm.

"She is probably in the last place I was, in a cage far below the palace. That is all I know," Zinn says, shaking out of my grip.

"What do you mean by a cage?" I say. Anger is clouding my vision.

"What is going on, Sonny? Isn't this who we have come for?" he asks, confused, glancing back and forth between Zinn and me.

"No, it is the wrong girl," I say, full of frustration.

"We cannot linger here. The door will be closing soon. You must go if you want to save the girl you have come for," the old Fae says, urgency in his voice.

"Who are you?" Zinn questions the old Fae.

"Well, if you must call me something, you can call me Sky, but we really don't have time for any of this chatter," Sky points out, nodding to the slowly closing door.

"Shit. You are sure that Nix is in there, Zinn?" I ask Zinn, watching my window of time closing quickly.

"Yes, now I have to go," Zinn says.

"Curse you, Zinn. Your very existence sickens me," I say, rushing to the door. As I rush towards the door, a large figure's frame comes into view, and before I know what is happening, I am punched with a force I have never felt before and black out.

NIX

I breathe out and find I am lying on the hard, cold ground. My body aches in ways I never thought possible. What is going on? Where am I? I open my eyes, take in my surroundings, and realize, with dread, that I know exactly where I am. No. Not here, not now. I can't be here. How did she do it? I have been trying for days to enter her mind, and she has made us switch places. How? I run to the cage door and am met with a severe and sharp electric shock. I can't be here, no, no, no.

"Ana! Ana, I am in here. Can you hear me?" I scream, but I get no reply.

"Brone!" I scream.

"Can anybody hear me? May? It's Nix. I am in here," I scream at the top of my lungs.

No one comes. Can anyone even hear me? How long will it take them to realize that we have switched places? I try to blast the door open with Wind, but nothing happens, and I realize the cage was enchanted specifically against Zinn's magic. So why won't mine work here? I try again, but nothing. The thought of having to be locked in Zinn's cage, powerless, fills me with dread.

ANA

Shit. Shit. Shit. What am I going to say? What am I going to do? Where could Nix have gone in such a hurry? I come to the foot of the throne, curtsy low, and Lord Stick-Up-His-Butt nods in acknowledgment.

"My Lord. It appears that Nix has disappeared somewhere in the palace. She has run off, and even Brone couldn't find her. I have had Brone notify the staff to search the palace. She should be returned shortly," I say with my head bowed for once to Lord Stick-Up-His-Butt.

"I see. That was the most unpleasant display she made as she ran off. I thought you had things under control?" Lord Stick-Up-His-Butt says with lightly veiled anger.

"I do, I mean, I did. I am not sure what happened. One minute we were dancing, then she, well, she just took off. I am not sure what happened, my Lord," I say, trying to keep my shit together.

"She had better be found. Maybe I have been giving her too many liberties to wander the palace. You will be held responsible if something has happened to her," Lord Stick-Up-His-Butt responds to my jumbled sentence, then waves his hand at me to dismiss me.

I wait on the side of the throne. It has been fifteen minutes, and still no sign of Brone. This is not good. Not good at all. Another eternity passes, and suddenly a boom sounds across the ballroom as the large door bangs open. Relief hits me. Brone found her. The throng of Fae that continued their revelry since Nix's exit stops to look at the sound. As the Fae part for Brone to come to the throne, my heart plummets. I see he doesn't have Nix, but has a human boy. The boy has a newly forming black eye and struggles in Brone's grip.

"Who are you?" Lord Stick-Up-His-Butt demands, letting his glamor pheromones seep out towards the young man.

"Cadmun," is all he replies, still struggling in Brone's strong grip.

Oh my Spirits. This is him, the boy that Nix has been worried about. But how did he even get to the Great Tree? Only Fae can find it. What is he doing here?

"Why are you here?" Lord Stick-Up-His-Butt presses.

"I have come to save Nix from all of you," Cadmun states, plainly defiant in his eyes. Lord Stick-Up-His-Butt chuckles a little, the sound unpleasant.

"How did you get here? Did you have help?" Lord Stick-Up-His-Butt continues his questioning.

"I came with the old Fae from under the hill, Sky is his name," Cadmun responds, with obvious fear in his eyes. "Where is she? Tell me. I must see Nix," he continues, fighting hard in Brone's tight grip.

"Stop struggling," Lord Stick-Up-His-Butt commands, and Cadmun falls still, then Briar continues. "Well, thank you for your cooperation. Brone, please remove this filth from my sight and place him with our other special guest. Ana see to our new guest. You know what to do," Lord Stick-Up-His-Butt commands, and Brone quickly ushers Cadmun away.

Shit. What is going on? Where the fuck is Nix? I have so many questions about what is happening, I quickly double-time it to catch up with Brone. We make our way out of the ballroom and take the winding hallways down to the lower levels of the palace until we reach the door to Zinn's dungeon. Brone throws open the door, dragging Cadmun into the room. Brone tosses Cadmun to the floor, then binds him to the ground with tightly woven vines and gags him as well.

"ANA! Help me!" Zinn cries out in desperation.

"What do you want, Zinn? If you can't tell, I have other problems right now," I say, dismissing her plea.

"No, Ana, it's me, Nix. Zinn did something, and we traded places. Please let me out," she chokes out on a sob.

"I don't have time to play games. Don't you see that I have something else to deal with right now?" I tell her that I'm getting irritated.

"Now, why are you here?" I turn to Cadmun, spilling glamor out towards him to pull the truth out of him. Then I nod to Brone to release the gag he placed over his mouth.

"I am here to save Nix, I told you that. Nix! Nix! It is me, Cadmun. I am here now. Are you ok?" he shouts towards Zinn.

"Cadmun! Is it really you?" she chokes out.

"Hush, Zinn. This has nothing to do with you," I shoot at her.

"But I am telling you it is me, Ana. Zinn and I switched places. Just look at me, I am sure you will be able to tell—my eyes. My eyes have changed. I know it," she pleads.

"I will do anything to shut you up," I say, turning toward the cage and slowly walking toward it.

"Hurry, please. Get me out of here," she begs.

As I approach, my irritation grows from her pleading. I have to figure out exactly how Cadmun even found the Great Tree. I don't need this distraction. I look up at Zinn, who is looking back at me with kyanite-blue eyes.

Oh fuck.

ZINN

"Hurry now, girl!" Sky says, beckoning me to come.

As I watch Brone knock Cadmun to the ground, I am struck by the urge to go to Cadmun's aid. Brone looks me in the eyes, shakes his head no, then mouths the word,

"Run."

That is exactly what I do. Sky grabs hold of my arm, and we are both propelled by a strong Wind, hurrying our steps to an inhuman speed—the greenery parts for us. Our pace never slows for what feels like an eternity. My shoulder is aching, and I need a rest, at least to get out of this god-awful gown.

"Stop, please stop," I say, breathless. I come to such a fast stop that I tumble to the ground, landing on my bad shoulder.

"Oh fuck," I cry out as I feel pain radiate from my injury.

"Come on, girl, we have to keep moving!" Sky says in an impatient tone.

"Well, my name isn't girl, it is Zinn, and don't you think we could go much faster if I get this damn dress off?" I huff back at him and start trying to get out of the stupid gown.

I am struggling with the thick fabric. Sky hands me a knife he pulled from his boot. I use it to shred the dress's bodice and pull it off. Then, I make quick work of removing the many layers of skirts until I am left in a plain cotton shift. I toss the knife back to Sky. I tear some of the fabric from the pile of ruined material and wrap my bad arm in a sling.

"Thanks, I am ready to go," I say, facing Sky, who nods at me in approval.

We take off again at breakneck speed and keep going until the sun is high in the sky. I am pleasantly surprised that the magic I pull from the Wind hasn't tired me at all. Sky holds out his arm, and we come to a sudden stop.

"It is best we find a place to sleep," he says, surveying the trees around us.

"No, I don't need a rest, we can keep going," I reply, bouncing on the balls of my feet, feeling like I need to put as much space as humanly possible from that place.

"No, we will be less visible in the trees during the day. We can move more easily in the cover of night. Besides, there are always more Seekers in the day than at night. Besides, most Seekers never think to look up," Sky says, still looking at the trees, then points to one and says, "Here, this one will be good, lots of foliage we can blend right in."

"Blend in? How? Are you sure we shouldn't keep moving?" I question him, fear clawing at my back.

"Yes, trust me, this is the safest course of action. We can also form a plan," Sky says and begins to scale the tree.

I watch as he climbs with expertise I wouldn't have expected from such an old-looking man, well, I guess Fae. I am unsure if I should follow him and climb the tree or make a run for it on my own.

"Don't even think about it, girl. You will only get lost. Better get climbing if you want to get some rest. You will need it. We have a long road before us yet," Sky says, seeming to know more than he is saying.

"Fine," I huff and take off my sling since my arm seems to finally be healed from whatever I did to it in the library. I stuff the strip in my shirt's pocket and make my way up the tree.

I sit on a large branch below Sky, and I scoot back to the tree's trunk and settle in. Who is this male, anyway, and why is he helping me? My mind is finally catching up to what is happening right now. Why should I trust this Fae with my safety? He was with Cadmun, but that doesn't mean much if

Nix was their goal. My curiosity and anxiety are mixing in the pit of my stomach, making me nauseous.

"Who are you really?" I question Sky.

"Well, as I told you, I am Sky, or as others call me, 'the man under the hill'," he replies, and sketches a bow. Acting as if what he just said should mean something to me.

Then it hits me like a wave. Nix's memories flood my mind.

***

The sight of Jameson's corpse. Nix is pulling in the power from the mirror—Cadmun's kiss. Nix and Cadmun are entering the wood. The letter from Fiona that Nix barely read because it was addressed to me. The directions to the man under the hill were the only part she read properly. Brone is capturing her. Her fear for Cadmun is so strong I can taste it. Nix being told she was a princess. Oh my Spirits, the truth about Ana and the revelation that I really am the reason they became friends. The utter hopelessness of being alone in the world. The confusion. Her feeling that she doesn't know who she really is. The pain of what I have done to her heart is turning her heart hard. The anger. The rage, but the freedom.

Lord Briar's lessons with May. The way my Spirit made her feel so much euphoria. I have never known such pleasure. Nix is trying to enter my mind, but she only finds a wall of darkness. Lord Briar whispers to her how she will become the ruler of everything. Then the dancing, and then the shift.

I am thrown completely back into the present,

"Oh no, Nix," I whisper. Nix is my last thought before I black out.

NIX

The last thing I see is Ana's eyes. Things start to go dark, and all I hear is someone saying,

"Hurry, get the key!" Then I am spiraling down, down, down into darkness.

I am watching through Zinn's eyes: Daniel, his topaz eyes. My body tingles at his touch. I want to see that hundred-watt smile. The urgency to see him and feel the touch of his hand, feather-light on mine. I want to kiss him into oblivion—the feeling of being complete. If there were only one star left in the sky, it would be him. Daniel. In Daniel's black Subaru, the box is in my hands, tucking it away under the seat. The fun of dyeing my hair black as a fuck you to Nix. The satisfaction from punching Seth in his smug face. My voice was strong and steady, singing to Ana and Daniel with abandon. A white fox was in the road, and then the crash—a cloth covering my face. Darkness consumed me, then I woke in a cage. Ana's incessant questioning is making my body writhe—the pain of the whip biting into my soft flesh. Then the agony of my Spirit seeps out of me, and I watch it fill Nix. I feel everything, and my nerve endings scream in agony. Protecting those I love, but still thinking I deserve the pain.

***

I suck in a labored breath, I am aching all over, then my eyes flutter open.

"Ana, the box. Daniel has the box. It is in his car. Zinn put it under the seat. I saw her do it," I say with labored breaths, still feeling phantom pains throughout my entire body. I roll to my side and wretch.

"Nix, are you ok? What just happened?" Ana says, gently rubbing my back.

"What have you done to her? Get off of her!" I hear Cadmun shouting, and look to see him fighting his bindings.

I wipe my mouth with the back of my hand, sit up slowly, and see that I am still inside Zinn's cage. The door is open, and look and see Cadmun struggling in the corner.

Brone looks on in judgment. Ana is on the ground with me, and worry lines her face.

"Did I do well? I saw it for you, Ana. Zinn hurts so much," my voice breaks off with a sob.

"Stop what you are doing to her!" Cadmun demands again, pulling even harder to be free from his bonds.

"Oh, Nix, yes, you did so well. Are you ok? What is happening?" Ana says, comfortingly.

"Her memories came all at once," I say, wincing a little.

"Brone, secure the prisoner in the cage and glamor him silent. We must notify Briar of what has happened," Ana says urgently, fear lacing her tone.

Brone puts Cadmun in the cage, orders him to be silent, and then exits the room.

"Come sit over here, Nix," she says

Ana pulls the chair towards me, and I weakly stand and climb into it. I haven't felt so weak in days. Is this what it feels like not to have my power from Zinn? I am not sure I like this empty feeling.

"Is it always like that when you change places?" Ana asks with worry in her voice.

"No. It has never been like that, but it has been such a long time since we switched," I reply, my body feeling the aftershocks of the pain Zinn experienced.

"What is the meaning of this? Why would you call me here? I do not have time for your failures, Ana," Lord Briar admonishes Ana.

"Please, my Lord, I do not understand what is going on. I was dancing with Nix in the ballroom, and then she took off. When we came to secure the boy, we found Nix in the cage, not Zinn. I don't know what has happened," Ana pleads.

Briar approaches Ana and gives her a sharp slap across her face, splitting her lip.

"No, please don't blame Ana, my Lord. It had to be Zinn who orchestrated this. It isn't Ana's fault," I say desperately.

"Well, for you, Dearest One, I will refrain from further punishment. Still, things have changed. We must change your appearance, or the court will become suspicious. I think I know just the thing. Want to play a game, Dearest One?" Lord Briar says, wickedness shining through his eyes, "Brone, go get the girl the Seekers found in the Wood."

Minutes tick by, and tension grows in the room. I have no idea what is going on. What girl is he talking about? Did they already capture Zinn? If they did, why would they not have brought her here?

The door opens, and Brone is dragging a resisting girl into the room. I see her clearly as they reach the center of the room, and I recognize her: Echo, the girl from Bleaker. I don't know her well at all, and I don't know how she even ended up here. Brone roughly shoves her to the ground and tells her to stay and be silent and still in what I now recognize as a glamoured voice.

"Brone, take the prisoner from the cage," Lord Briar commands, and Brone stalks to the cage, roughly pulls Cadmun from the cage, and shoves him to the floor next to Echo. Then Brone commands him to stay as well.

Apprehension fills me as Lord Briar turns to me and levels me with an evil stare, raising the hairs on the back of my neck.

"Now, Dearest One, we are going to play our game. Choose," he says, nodding towards Cadmun and Echo.

"What do you mean?" I ask, confused.

"You are weak and need to refill your energy. Choose whose Spirit you will take. The boy or the girl? Who will you choose? Either way, you will be rewarded. So who is it to be?" He says, eyes full of curiosity.

Dread fills me. How am I supposed to choose? Draining Zinn made sense. She deserved it. But, as I look into the fear-filled eyes of Echo and Cadmun, I am not sure I can do it. But I feel weak, and my body is calling out, feeling the pull of Spirit radiating from Cadmun and Echo. I think of

Cadmun and all we have been through, but I know he is strong, gifted with the elements like no other. I turn to Echo and feel no attachment to her, and she is definitely the weaker of the two.

Conflicted, I look between the two of them. I raise my hand and direct it at Cadmun, knowing I am moments away from feeling relief from the emptiness I feel from no longer having Zinn's power. His power calls to me, and I keep my hand directed at Cadmun and begin pulling the Spirit from him. Relief washes over me. Suddenly, I am filled with the memory of us in the shed, him crying. The kiss, and I quickly redirect my hand to Echo. I pull with all my power and watch as she lifts from the floor, and she begins to wither away, a scream escaping her lips. I pull and pull, and exquisite power fills me, and I damn the consequences that may come. Echo's final breath comes, and I reach a level of power that I never did with Zinn. Echo falls to the floor, eyes staring blindly into my soul, and I feel a moment of regret. I look to Cadmun, who is staring at me with absolute horror in his eyes, then shakes his head in disbelief. Maybe even judgment?

"Maybe not the choice I would have made, but I did promise you a reward. You may keep the boy as your gift from me. Mind that he behaves. Glamor him if you must, so you keep him under control. You did well, my Dearest One." Lord Briar says, then he sweeps from the room.

I fall to my knees and let the power flow through me. My ears shift back to point, my vitality returns, and my hair, which has fallen forward, slowly changes back to snow white. I have never experienced such divine pleasure. Draining Zinn felt good, but completely draining a Spirit feels even better.

ANA

I am dumbfounded by what I just witnessed. I watch as Brone gently picks up Echo's lifeless body. His face looks pained. He glances toward Nix, and his eyes glow with simmering hatred. How? How could Nix do it? She drained the poor girl to death. This isn't the sweet Nix I love. I watch as she stands and glides toward Cadmun.

"You are mine now," she says with slight relief but also a possessiveness that makes me shiver. "Ana, come with me. I will need to bathe and change. How do I get Cadmun to follow? I am not sure how glamor works." She looks at me with expectant eyes.

I hesitate slightly before I explain how glamor works.

"Well, it comes from inside you. You must say what you want your target to do with clear intentions. As you focus on your intent, draw in a breath, then release your desired outcome. Your Fae power should do the rest," I instruct her, feeling like she shouldn't add this power to her arsenal.

"Cadmun, come," Nix says, a sweet smell releasing from her. It almost seems to call me to her as well. Cadmun rises quickly. Nix turns to the door, and he obediently follows her. I have to restrain myself from taking a step toward her. Just how powerful is she becoming?

"Ana, are you coming?" Nix questions, and we leave the prison behind us. I find myself walking into a future I don't think I want.

CADMUN

Nix turns toward me, and I don't know who I am looking at anymore, and it's making my heart ache for the girl who sings songs about only needing love.

I am being pulled along not of my own volition. I never thought I would witness Nix do something so cold. The sound of Echo's scream is still ringing in my ears. I watch Nix's back and notice new scars crisscrossing all over it. What have they been doing to her? How is she so changed? We reach a large door with naked Fae carved all over it, and Nix pushes her way into the room as I follow. I see we are in a large bathing room. As other Fae see Nix enter, some gasp.

"Leave," Nix says in a commanding voice, and they all do. Leaving their discarded clothing, departing as fast as they can.

"Ana, can you get me fresh clothes?" Nix says and starts stripping out of her dirty white shift.

I am shocked and try to turn my back on Nix to give her privacy, but I am frozen in place by the glamour she holds over me. Heat rises in my cheeks as I see her nude form. I close my eyes, feeling like I am seeing something I shouldn't.

"You can look if you like, Cadmun," Nix says softly, but her voice carries due to the acoustics of the room. "Oh, and you may speak if you wish," her voice full of a sweet aroma hits me.

"What is going on, Nix? I came here to help you, but you don't seem… well, to be yourself." I say in a rush of words, keeping my eyes closed.

"Well, what do you mean by 'yourself'? Do you even know who I am?" Nix replies as I hear the water splashing.

"You know what I mean," I say, frustration lacing my words.

"Oh, do I?" Nix questions.

"Yes. Where is the girl I know? The girl who couldn't stand the idea of turning into Mod or Jameson? Because where I am sitting, it seems that that girl is gone," I say, my eyes snapping open. She slightly flinches at my words, but schools her features into a quick mask of cool indifference. "Well, you know me, if you don't know yourself. When have I ever questioned your intentions? What you did to Echo was wrong. You know that, don't you? You seem more like Zinn than yourself. Zinn would snap up power in a second. But not you, Little Flower."

"What do you know of me, Cadmun? I was under Zinn's thumb since we first met, and now that I am free from her, you choose to judge me so quickly?" Nix asks, something dark lurking behind her eyes.

"You always wanted to be free from her, but did you want to become heartless? You know what the curse on the land does, or did you forget that as well as who you are?" I shoot at her, seeing a fraction of that darkness fade.

The door opens, and I see the girl Nix called Ana enter with a middle-aged, brown-haired woman carrying a luxurious white and light blue gown. Nix stands, and water sluffs down her body as she does. I look at my feet.

"Cadmun, our conversation is over for now," Nix says in a tone that I now know is full of glamour.

The frustration of being cut off makes my fists clench. Nix dresses quickly, and the middle-aged woman braids half her hair, then sweeps it around her head into what looks like a crown, placing small jeweled pins in it. Nix pulls vines with her power from the wall of the room, and they wrap around her arms, then says,

"Much better."

I realize I have no idea who the girl standing in front of me is anymore.

ZINN

I wake suddenly to a light touch on my arm.

"You alright, girl? Where did you go just now?" Sky asks with concern in his eyes.

"Yes, I am fine, just give me a second. My sister's memories just came flooding back to me. It has never happened like that before," I say, pulling myself together.

"Does it happen often?" Open curiosity is in Sky's voice

"Not like that. It has been a long time since we switched places, so that must be why it hit so hard," I tell Sky, not knowing why I am trusting him with all this information.

"Hmm… I think you may be onto something, girl," Sky answers, tapping his chin with his finger.

"Who are you? Why are you helping me? I am nobody to you?" I ask, not knowing what to make of the old Fae before me.

"Maybe nobody to me, but you are somebody to someone," Sky says in a weird riddle.

"What does it matter? That somebody isn't anywhere I can go," I say, toying with the necklace, thinking of Daniel.

Nix must know where the mirror is by now, and there is nothing I can do to protect him from here.

"What is that you have there?" Sky says, looking down from his branch to examine the necklace Ana gave me, well, I guess she gave Nix, really. My heart still hurts that Ana was never really my friend.

"Oh, this was a gift," I say, and he reaches down and pulls the necklace from my neck. Then he smashes the stone against the tree. "Hey, what the fuck?" I say, surprised by his sudden destruction of the necklace, but a slight fog lifts from my mind.

"Whoever gave you that is no friend of yours. That carried bad magic. It looks like the sorcerer's stone, but that was a fake. Did you see how easily it broke? That stone will only bring what you want most in the worst way," Sky says, warning in his tone.

"What is that supposed to mean?" I ask, getting impatient with his riddle talk.

"That stone brings subtle emotions and makes them stronger than they should be. It is a trickster, a master manipulator making us feel things that are true but also not real," Sky says, repositioning himself onto his branch.

"Whatever you say, riddle master," I say, flustered by the way he words things.

A twig snaps, and Sky's hand shoots down, covering my mouth. He slowly nods in the direction of the noise, and a trio of Fae comes into sight: a blond, a redhead, and one with horns. We watch from our hiding place as they pass, talking in low voices. They pass as quickly as they came, but I don't let the air out of my lungs until Sky removes his hand from my mouth.

"Who were they?" I ask nervously.

"Seekers, but they don't seek animals. They hunt the humans that enter the Wood. That ridiculous trial you humans think you need to do to prove your dominance over the Wood. I have saved many humans over the years, but some fall through the cracks. Seekers are rewarded with Spirit from each human they catch. The worst is when they find the babes your people leave to die in the Wood. Those are the hardest to lose to Briar, only to grow up and be slaves to his court. I cannot save them all," he says, sadness written on his face. "There is a haven in the Wood I have made for those of your kind I can save. I take the babes there to be watched over by the older humans. I concealed the haven from all other Fae. It cost me a lot of my own Spirit to make, but all magic comes at a cost." Sky looks at me with trust in his eyes as he tells me his secrets.

"So not all of them die?" I ask, with hope filling my heart, that there is some goodness left in this world.

"No, girl, none of them die, but the ones I can't save become beholden to the Lord of the Wood," he says as if it should be common knowledge.

"My name is Zinn," I bark at him with a little too much bite, but it is my name, and I want to hear it. I never want to be called Nix again in my life.

"Ok, ok, calm down, young one. I will use your name if I must. I don't like to get attached to you, young folk. There was one girl I did become fond of that may be of interest to you," Sky says, mischief in his voice.

"Who would that be? Your girlfriend? I am good. I don't need to know about that," I say, feeling slightly grossed out.

"No, Zinn, not a lover, but your mother, Fiona," he says, and I freeze.

"What do you know about my mother?" I say, my voice darkening.

"Well, she looks like a young one of long ago, Edwon? Edween? Edwin? I forget his name, but his name matters not. Fiona found her way through the Wood where she met your father," he says solemnly, shaking his head slightly in disapproval.

"You mean Lord Briar?" I ask my mouth, feeling dry.

"Yes, Zinn. Fiona was one of a kind. She had a beauty that even rivaled that of the Fae. Her magic was just as powerful as the Fae, unpolluted by Spirit magic. Lord Briar was captivated by her. I thought she would shift the balance, but alas, that wasn't what turned out in the end," Sky says sadly.

"What do you mean by the balance?" I ask, confused.

"You must know of the curse, do you not? The land was tainted by a curse long ago, and we all still suffer from its effects," he replies, bowing his head, sadness in his eyes.

"Yes, I know about the curse and that draining Spirit magic will cost, your very goodness," I say and shiver, remembering my very own Spirit being pulled from my body and Nix's changed appearance.

"Well, there was a flaw, you see, when Thorne cursed the land and ordered the Fae back to the Wood. It had a cost, and that cost was empathy. The Fae also lost their ability to empathize with the humans. The Fae came to believe they were superior in every way. That way of thinking has endured. So, when Fiona came along and caught the attention of Lord Briar, I thought all would be set right. I was wrong," he says sadly.

"What do you mean? What happened?" I am hungry for more information about my mother.

"Lord Briar wanted her to start draining other humans to gain even more power, but she refused him. But it was too late for her at that point, she had fallen pregnant. She made her escape and came to me. I helped her the best I could, but in the end, she still died," he says, chilling me to the bone.

"But, why? Why did she die?" I ask, tears filling my eyes.

"Because of you, Zinn. She died to protect you and your sister. She created strong magic to protect you two, and that always comes at a cost. She drained parts of your Spirits, tethering them to the mirrors with love. I helped her craft them. It is very strong but tricky magic. She was weakened by it and would not have been able to fight against your father, so she did the only thing she could do to protect you both. She took her own life to keep you both secret and safe," he finishes quietly.

I knew how this story would end, but I never wanted to believe that Fiona had taken her own life. But now I know that it is true. Fiona did it to keep us safe. The sky is starting to darken, and I look up to see a glorious field of stars unfolding.

"But why didn't the curse break? Wouldn't a mother's love be the purest?" I ask, confused.

"Ah, you would think so, but remember, she drained yours and your sister's Spirits to create the mirrors, corrupting her own soul. Only someone untouched by the corruption that kind of magic creates can break the curse that lies in the world of Bleaker and the Wood. Also, I realized too late she was not of Thorne's lineage," he tells me, then continues, saying, "Ok, time to go, Zinn." Sky says, waving his hands and undoing his magic on the vines around us.

"Time to go where?" I question reeling from all this information.

"Well, to the safe haven, of course. Not even Lord Briar can touch you there." He says as he climbs down the tree.

"What? I can't go there. I need to get back to Nix's world," I say, thinking of Daniel.

"Why would you need to go there?" Sky asks, with a knowing look in his crystal-clear blue eyes.

"There is someone there I need to help if I can get there in time," I reply, hoping that he will help me.

"Ah, I see," he says, scratching the back of his neck, considering what I have just said.

"Will you help me? I don't know how to get there. But there must be a way," I say urgently.

"There is a way," a gravelly voice says behind me, and I turn to see him. Brone. The one who tortured me, the one who kissed me, but also the one who helped me run.

BRONE

I am hit with the strongest gust of Wind to the gut, I have ever felt. I land flat on my back, the wind knocked out of me. I feel vines creep all around my body, pinning me to the hard earth. I do not fight, not this time. I surrender. Consequences be damned, I no longer wish to serve Lord Briar as long as I live.

"What do you want, servant of darkness?" Sky demands, and I realize he is my captor.

"I am not here to fight, not this time. I am here to assist in any way I can," I reply sincerely.

"How could you help? All you do is Lord Briar's bidding!" Sky says, losing his usual composure.

"I can help Zinn. I can help her get to the human world. I know the way," I say calmly.

"I can help her just as well as you could, you brute," Sky says, sounding slightly offended.

"Let her choose," I say, hoping I am making the right decision.

"Why should I choose? Why would you even offer to help? All you know is how to torture," Zinn says, voice unsure.

My heart begins to sink. Maybe I was wrong to come. I couldn't be a part of whatever Lord Briar's plan is any longer. I was told to find Zinn but not bring her back. As long as he hasn't caught on, I will not be affected by my blood oath to him.

"They will be sending more Seekers to find you. I am the best one Lord Briar has, and your best chance to get where you want to go," I tell Zinn, craning my head so I can look into her eyes. I see it. That look of fire and defiance was dancing in her beautiful gray eyes. The sight ignites the fire of my own defiance.

"Oh, you're the best, huh? That is your reasoning?" Zinn says, sarcasm dripping from her lips.

"Yes, and if we play it right, maybe Sky could misdirect the other Seekers. I can take secret routes and keep them off our trail. I know how they operate since I trained them. So, you see, I am your best choice if you really wish to save whoever it is you love," I tell her, hoping she will choose me.

"So, if I don't choose you. Will you give away our plan?" Zinn asks, worry lighting her eyes.

"No, but I will not be able to distract the other Seekers like Sky can. He knows the Wood better than anyone.

He knows how to blend in, distract, and fool other Fae. Sky has been doing it for a very long time to save your people," I say, directing my gaze towards Sky, his eyes full of untold secrets.

"Zinn, the Seeker is right," Sky relents, his shoulders slightly slumping in defeat.

"But how can I trust him?" Zinn asks Sky, obviously valuing his opinion over my logic, which stings.

"Zinn, there are many things at stake right now. I will help you, but it is your choice. Choose wisely and choose carefully," Sky says with weight filling his words.

"Will you promise to keep the other Seekers off our trail?" Zinn asks him.

"Yes, you have my word," Sky replies seriously.

"And you promise this isn't a trick, Brone?" Zinn directs at me.

"It is no trick," I reply in earnest.

"Ok, Brone, I will go with you. You let me run when you could have stopped me. Thank you," her thanks freely given chips at my heart, "but betray me, and I will end you," she says, not breaking her gaze from mine.

"Brone, I will be off now. I assume the other Seekers were not far behind you," Sky says, and releases the vines he had been binding me to the ground. "Zinn, the path before you is not set in stone. The very Wood is waiting for your final choice. Be wary of the bond that has you bound," Sky says and takes off, pushing himself with a strong gust of Wind.

"Wait, what do you mean?" Zinn calls after him, but he is gone.

NIX

"Dearest One, I have a task for you. You must go to the human realm and retrieve the mirror left there. Ana will accompany you. You Nix must remain hidden. Let no one see you. Strange Fae are lurking about Hawthorn, and this will raise suspicion among humans. Once you retrieve the mirror, you must clean up Ana's mess and wipe all evidence of your existence. Be smart. Stay alert and return as soon as you are done," Lord Briar says to me, and I nod in acknowledgment.

Lord Briar takes a necklace with the fairy teleportation charm I now recognize from Zinn's memories, from his robe's pocket. He steps behind me, places it around my throat. I feel his breath on my neck, and the hairs on my nape stand on end. He places a matching charm into Ana's hand, and she fastens it around her own neck.

"Come, Ana, let's go," I tell her, then turn to Cadmun and send a wave of glamour at him, "Cadmun, go to my chambers and remain there until my return."

I take the hood of the black cloak I am wearing, pull it over my head, and hide my face deep within its folds. I take Ana's hand and nod that I am ready. She nods in return, closes her eyes in concentration, and we are transported in a beautiful kaleidoscope of swirling colors. The beauty of it takes my breath away. Magic always surprises me with its beauty. Before I have the time to fully appreciate it, my feet land hard on the pavement of the sidewalk in front of Daniel's house. When I glance at the driveway, I don't see his black Subaru parked in it.

"Shit, the car isn't here," Ana says in frustration. Dropping my hand quickly, she walks to peer inside the front window, "Nope, he definitely isn't here, the house is all dark. Where could he be?"

"Where else—at Hawkes?" That is where he and his cronies are always hanging out. Let's check there, I saw Zinn put it under the seat. It must still be there," I say, reaching for her. She withdraws slightly, and I see her shiver. Then she grasps my hand in hers slowly.

Once again, we are transported on the kaleidoscope of swirling colors and land outside the sports bar. I scan the parking lot and spot it, the black Subaru. Ana and I approach it carefully, so we won't be seen. I pull at the passenger door handle, the door opens, and I smile, knowing everyone in this small town would never even think of locking their car doors. I bend down, reaching deeply under the seat, and feel nothing. No box. No mirror.

"It isn't here, Ana. I know I saw her put it in his car. It should be right here. Check the back," I command Ana as I search the front more thoroughly. I even open the glovebox, but find nothing.

"Nothing back here either. Damn it," Ana says, flustered.

"So, I see you have come to play," a silky voice comes from behind me, and I turn, suddenly ready for a fight. I recognize the two girls standing in front of me. Zinn met them. With my new understanding of how the Fae power feels, I can see as clearly as day that the duo are Fae.

"What do you want?" I ask in a demanding tone. Ana and I are here on a mission and don't have time for this.

"Why are you two here?" Ana asks, seeming to know them.

"We like it here. We come to play with the locals. It is just so easy to get here through the portal in the Wood by that little town, Bleaker. Not to mention that boy Seth tastes wickedly good," the shorter girl, I think, is named Ivy, says.

"Lord Briar will like to know what you two have been up to, I am sure of it. I'll be sure to tell him," Ana threatens.

The taller girl lets out a hiss, showing fangs, and launches toward Ana. I don't have time to think. I reach out my hand and start pulling on her Spirit. I am filling up on the sweet taste of power, potent in her Fae blood. It is so much richer than Echo's Spirit. Ivy lets out a screech, lunges at me, and my other hand raises to catch her around her throat. She struggles and rips out a handful of my hair. I close my grip tighter around her throat. At our sudden skin contact, Ivy's Spirit begins to flow into me as well. I think I hear Ana saying something like 'no, stop,' but I don't pay any attention to her. I am consuming them simultaneously, and it is like I know exactly who I am at this moment: Nix, princess of the Wood, all-powerful Fae. The flow of Spirit trickles off, and I release Ivy's body from my hand and let the other female fall to the ground as my pull releases her.

"What have you done, Nix?" Ana hisses at me, fear shining in her eyes. I look down and see the withered corpses of the two Fae on the ground. Did I do that? I took it without needing permission. I feel the power coursing through me, letting me know every second of it was real.

"I thought they were going to attack you, so I just acted. What does it matter? They aren't supposed to be here, right? I just saved us, Ana. I don't see the problem here," I hiss back.

"Well, what are we supposed to do now?" Ana asks with anxiety in her voice.

"We are supposed to find the box, right, so let's start with that," I say as if it weren't obvious.

"I meant about the mess you just made here," Ana says, pointing at the Fae's bodies.

"I don't care. You handle it. I am going back to Daniel's house to see if the box is there," I say, and turn and walk to the edge of the parking lot and teleport. Just as I am about to evaporate from view, I see Daniel walking out of the bar looking miserable. I see him, and I feel nothing but disgust.

Arriving back at Daniel's, I walk up to the front door, check the knob, and just like the car, it is unlocked. I follow the path to his room, given to me from Zinn's memories, and walk in. There, right on top of his desk, is the mirror, the box, a small blue bag that used to contain the necklace I am wearing, and two small bundles of hair, one white, one black. I rush over and snatch the mirror off the desk and pop it open. I open it quickly and discover it is broken, no glass remains. I pace the room for a few minutes, wondering what to do now. What will Lord Briar do? I hear feet approaching me, and I will myself out of the house back to the bar.

"Nix," I hear my name whispered.

I turn to look to see who is calling my name and see Ana crouching down beside a car I don't recognize, waving for me to come to her. I stow the broken mirror in my pocket, and Ana quickly wills us to the clearing behind the elementary school.

"What did you do with the bodies?" I ask Ana, and she points over my shoulder.

"I teleported them here. I'm not sure what to do," Ana says nervously.

"Well, we still need to glamour the town. Maybe we can make it so the people don't see the bodies as well," I suggest.

"Yeah, that could work, let's just do that," Ana says, shoulders relaxing slightly.

"Ok, let's do it already," I tell Ana impatiently.

"Take both my hands. We will need to concentrate all of our energy and glamor and send it out to the city limits. We must feed the glamor until we feel it takes hold of the people here. We will feel when the glamour is complete because the flow will automatically stop on its own once everyone's minds have been erased," Ana says.

"What about Amanda? Will she remember me?" I ask quietly.

"No, Nix, no one will, not even Amanda. Even all the physical traces of you will disappear," Ana says, with a sad look in her eyes.

"Good. Let's be done with this town. My life is not here anymore," I say, and Ana flinches at my words.

As we hold hands, I feel glamour building inside of me. I send it out and erase every trace of me, every trace of Zinn. I also release all my memories tied to this place and these people. I feel the pull stop, and the world tilts, and I fall to my knees. Breathless, I pull my hood back, look up at the sky, and take my first breath of true freedom.

DANIEL

I walk into my room, and a hooded figure pockets the mirror, one of my only pieces of Nix. Could it be her? I whisper,

"Nix?"

I run toward the figure, but they vanish. I fall from the momentum and crash into my desk. I scramble up and look around my room, but I see no one. I look back at my desk, the box and blue bag, and bundles of hair lie there untouched, and a shiver runs through me. Someone was here. Why would anyone take the mirror, and more importantly, how did they vanish?

I take the box, then reach into my pocket, pull out the strange note I found in the mirror, and place it back inside. Excruciating pain shoots through me. It feels like needles are stabbing my eyes. I fall to my knees, dropping the box. I hold the sides of my head. The pain lasts for minutes, and then, just like that, it ends. When I look down, all that is left in front of me is a small pile of black hair. I search around with my hands, looking for the box and other items, but they are gone. I frantically search my floor methodically, and I come up with nothing. I only find the black bundle of hair and place it on my desk. What the hell is happening?

I stand up, shake off whatever that was, and realize it is time for me to head down to the police station. I have been going every evening to check the status of the ongoing cases related to the disappearances. Maybe it is my guilt about not reporting the items I found in my car to the police. That keeps me going back there every night, or my need to see her again. Now I am not even sure how to explain to the police that I had some of Nix's stuff, because it is gone.

I haven't been sleeping well since I broke the mirror. I always feel like I am buzzing with too much energy. Nix is circling through my head on a non-stop loop. I head back out to my car, pull up Spotify, and look for the Birthday Girl mix, but nothing comes up. I stare at my phone in disbelief. Did I accidentally delete it? Maybe that's it, but unease is sliding down my back.

I pull out of my driveway and make the short drive to the station in silence. I am becoming more and more weirded out as I notice all the missing-person fliers that were on nearly every tree and telephone pole are gone. I pull up, park, and notice there are far fewer cars and people coming and going from the station. Where are the FBI's unmarked cars? I walk apprehensively into the station and approach the front desk. All the case boards are empty, and only a raffle flier remains.

"Hey Rosey," I say to the front desk secretary-dispatcher for the whole Hawthorn police department.

"Oh, hello there, dear. Can I help you?" Rosey asks, looking at me like she hasn't ever seen me before.

"Hey, what is going on? Did something in the case change?" I ask my hands, feeling slick with sweat, so I rub them off on my jeans, and Rosey looks at me strangely.

"What case, dear?" She asks, arching her brows.

"Cases on Nix Smith's and Ana Burchard's disappearances," I say, my mouth feeling overly dry.

"Who now? We haven't had any missing person cases, well, now let me think. I actually can't think of a single one in my twenty-five years working here. Are you feeling ok there, dear? You look a little green around the gills," Rosey says, looking concerned.

"That can't be right. I have been coming here every day for weeks now. Are you sure there is nothing on the two missing girls?" I ask, starting to feel like I am going crazy.

"As I said, no one has been reported missing, dear," Rosey says, worry crossing her brow, "What was your name?" She asks, grabbing a Post-it note and a pen.

"Oh, I just, um, wanted to ask about the case. I see you are busy. I will just head out, sorry," I say, seeing that she wants to take down my information for some reason that has alarms going off in my head.

I climb back in my car and find myself feverishly scrolling through my phone and my recent texts. I pull up my pinned chats and see my whole text thread with Nix is missing. I pull up the contacts bar and type in 'Nix,' but no contact pops up. I delete her name from the search bar and enter 'Ana', and again, nothing. I switch to Google and type in 'Nix Smith Ana Burchard missing girls Hawthorn'. Google says no searches match. I am starting to panic. My breath is shallow. I look up and notice Rosey and an officer talking at the front door. She points towards me, and the officer looks. I put the keys in the ignition and drive away as quickly as I can without making a scene.

I need to find Seth. He must be doing this somehow. He is probably still at Hawkes waiting for those two girls he is always with now. I make my way back to the bar, sweating uncontrollably. I pull into the packed parking lot. It is summer after all, and Karaoke night. Karaoke night reminds me of the song Nix sang in her beautiful, haunting voice, capturing the whole bar's attention.

I head in the door, accidentally slamming it open, drawing attention to myself, and frantically searching the faces in the bar for Seth. I spot him near the dart boards and head over, shoving my way through the crowd, causing one girl to completely drop her beer on my way to get to him.

"Hey, watch it," she says, but I ignore her.

"Seth! What are you doing? How are you doing this?" I yell at him as I approach.

"Whoa. Daniel, are you ok? Not looking too good there, bro," he says, taking a swig of his beer.

"You know exactly what I am talking about. How are you doing this? I know you hated seeing me with her, but how did you make her disappear? I know it was you. You hated her. But why are you doing this to me?" I say, getting in his face.

"What are you talking about, bro? You need to back off," Seth says, standing and placing his beer next to a full cup of darts.

"Nix. You know the girl you loved calling 'Nix-aphrenia'? White hair, gray eyes. You made it part of your personal mission to make her life unbearable. Where is your phone? Give me your phone. You have a picture in there of her throwing up on that dance floor. Give it to me," I say, reaching out to snatch it from the table.

His hand gets there first, and he pockets it.

"You need to calm down, bro. I have no idea who you are talking about," he replies with a strange look in his eyes.

"See, you are just trying to hide your phone from me. Give it to me," I yell and knock his beer mug to the floor, and it shatters. Then I grab a dart from the now-spilled cup and launch it at the dartboard, causing the board to crack in half. I see the dart has punched halfway through the board and is now embedded in the wall, which is impossible. My ears are ringing loudly. I grab my head, and I feel weak. Then I am tackled to the ground, and I feel the sharp bite of the broken glass push into the soft flesh of my cheek.

"You are coming with us now, you need to calm down, or we will have to tase you," the stern voice of a cop demands.

CADMUN

I tug on the door to Nix's room, but it is bolted and won't budge. I punch the wood and leave a crack behind, and end up with bloody knuckles as my reward. Looking wildly around, I begin to search for anything I could use as a weapon. Pulling out the drawers of the dressers, I am only met with the sight of fine gowns and undergarments. I tear everything apart in my search, finding nothing useful. I pace around the room. I yell in frustration and knock the candlestick from the bedside table, and fall to my knees. I suddenly spot Nix's pack she brought from home. Rushing over, I dump all the contents and find only more clothing. I shake the bag one last time, and a small clinking sound comes from the floor. I spot a small glowing vial. I recognize it immediately and pocket it.

ZINN

We move swiftly and quietly through the Wood. Brone's back is to me, leading me back to Daniel. A tangle of anxiety knots in my stomach at the thought of what may have happened to him. The fairy charm necklace that Fiona left Nix in the human world gives Nix the advantage of speed. If something bad has happened to Daniel, I don't know what I will do. I don't know how I could make it right.

"The light is dwindling. We should rest for the night," I hear Brone's gravelly voice, and it clears my thoughts.

"Ok, so what tree looks good to you?" I ask, surveying the trees around us.

"We can't use the trees that will not keep us safe from those who seek us. We need deeper camouflage," Brone says, bending and placing his hand to the earth.

"Deeper? What the hell does that mean?" I say and then see the earth receding from his hand, hollowing out a large hole in the ground.

"We will be safer hidden in the ground than in the trees. After you," he says, nodding towards the hole in the ground. The thought of being trapped underground reminds me of my cage, and it fills me with dread.

"After you, my Lord," I say, extending my hand, not trusting him to lock me in that hole by myself.

"Don't address me with that name. Just call me Brone," he says, cutting me a severe glance. Then he deftly leaps into the hole.

I hesitate at the mouth of the hole. I take a large gulp of the fresh air and jump. I land wrong and almost fall, and strong arms wrap around me and steady me.

"Hey, hands off," I snap, still unsure if I should trust this male. His hands quickly leave my body, and I feel a small sense of loss from the gentle touch. No one has touched me gently in a long time.

Brone stalks over to the far corner of the hole and sits down. It looks like at least five people could comfortably fit in here, lying down. He pulls a small candle from his pack and lights it with a flame from his fingertip. He drops a small amount of wax on the ground and secures the candle's end to the dirt floor. Then he extends his hand and seals us in the hole.

He reaches into his pack again and pulls out fighting leathers, and I am filled with the urge to snatch them from him and get out of this filthy shift. As if reading my thoughts, he tosses them to me, which I snatch out of midair. Then he tosses some thin moccasin-style boots towards me as well. I take the supple leathers and tear off my shift, not caring that Brone is here, and begin to pull them on. They fit like a glove, and for the first time in a long time, I feel like something is right in the world.

"I have one last thing for you," he says, reaching into the pack and pulling out something wrapped in a dirty cloth and extending it toward me.

I take the bundle and open it to find six throwing daggers hidden in the folds of the cloth. Not just any throwing daggers, but my throwing daggers. I make quick work of slipping them into the sheaths strategically placed on my leathers, then sit down to put on the boots.

"Much better," Brone says, approval in his tone.

"I don't remember asking for your approval," I say, wanting to stick my tongue out at him like a child for some reason.

"I just meant that you look like the warrior you truly are," he says and clears his throat, shifting his position slightly as if nervous.

"What would you know about it?" I cut at him.

"Well, someone who endures great pain to protect the ones they love has the true soul of a warrior," he says with reverence, looking down at his hands.

I am stunned at his words. Quiet relief washes through me at his almost admission of the wrong he has done to me. I sit and look at him, wondering if I truly have a new ally.

"Hungry?" Brone asks a question, then tosses me some dried meat without waiting for my answer.

I tear into the morsel like an animal. The slop they kept feeding me in that cage may have kept me alive, but it tasted like dust in my mouth. This meat is the most delicious piece of food I have had in weeks. I moan in approval, and Brone looks at me with an unreadable look.

"What? If you were eating what I was every day, you would know how good it is to have real food," I say with my mouth full of meat.

"Once you finish, you should rest. We have a long day's travel before we reach the portal to the other realm," Brone tells me seriously.

"Another day! Can't we get there any faster?" I say, my anxiety for Daniel is spiking.

"We must be careful. The other Seekers will be in the Wood. We are heavily relying on Sky's distractions," Brone says, frustration laces his tone.

"I trust him. My mother trusted him. I know he won't let us down," I say with conviction.

"Rest now, Zinn. We will be safe here for the night," Brone says, stretching out on the ground and turning his back to me.

My nerves are on edge. I can't seem to fall asleep. This may be the last night I can get it, so I need to relax. I wait until I hear his breath even out and start to sing 'Lovely' by Billie Eilish to help calm the emotions welling up inside me. I finish the song, and my nerves finally settle, and I fall into a deep sleep.

NIX

Ana and I enter the ballroom and make eye contact with Lord Briar, and he nods, letting me know he has seen me. He stands, and all the Fae bow low, and I wonder what that would feel like to stop a room with one movement. Lord Briar descends from the throne and walks my way. He sweeps past me, and I move to follow him. We move through the great antechamber to the library. We cut through the center aisle, then turn left to his offices in the back. We all file into the luxurious space. Once the door closes, he turns and asks quickly,

"Did you find it, Dearest One?"

"Yes, but you may be disappointed," I say, worried about what his reaction will be.

"Disappointed? Why?" he says and glowers at Ana.

I pull the compact from my pocket and extend it to him. He swipes it out of my hand and opens it, and his eyes flare with anger. He casts it aside, and the sound of the metal on the tile floor is jarring. I prepare to be reprimanded, but Lord Briar walks past me and straight to Ana, beginning to drain her Spirit, only stopping once she is gasping for air.

"This is all your fault, if you had pulled the information from Zinn. This would never have happened. You are weak, and my patience for you is wearing thin," he turns to me, and I brace myself, ready to fight. I will not be subjected to anything that is not my fault.

"Dearest One, did you feel anything when you touched the mirror?" he asks, composing himself once more.

"No, my Lord. I felt nothing," I answer, still ready to defend myself if need be.

"I see. Well then, it seems the problem may have resolved itself. You see, we needed that mirror to unlock the rest of your power, but if nothing happened when you touched it, there must not have been any power imbued in it in the first place," he reasons and picking up, the mirror then placing it on top of a book I recognize as Cadmun's, then he continues, "Even if that is so, we still need your sister. I want you at full power before I announce you as my successor."

Successor, the word intoxicates me. Finally, someone sees me. I am not weak. I will not fade into the background. I will shine. I turn to Ana and see fear in her eyes, and I smile. Maybe she finally sees me, too.

"Dearest One, you may go. I need a word with Ana alone," he says with darkness in his eyes.

“Yes, my Lord,” I say, then turn to go, pausing to look at Ana, worried about her fate.

I walk out of the library and make my way to my chambers, where I know Cadmun will be waiting. What will he think about this new development? That I will become a Lady. Nix, Lady of the Wood, has a nice ring to it. I unlock the door and step inside to find Cadmun has gone through everything and left the room in disarray, and is currently lying in bed, staring at the ceiling.

“What have you done? You stay there,” I command, then turn back to the hallway and call out, “May! May! Where are you?”

A minute ticks by, and I am staring daggers at Cadmun, smirking at me from the bed. I hear hurried steps coming my way and turn to see May scurrying toward me.

“What took you so long?” I say impatiently.

“I am sorry, Mistress,” May says breathlessly.

“Look! Look what he has done, clean it up,” I demand, and she hurries into the room and begins cleaning it as quickly as possible.

“Wait, stop, Nix, don’t make her do it, I can,” Cadmun says, struggling to sit up, but can’t because of the glamour placed on him.

"Come, Cadmun. Keep your mouth shut," I say forcefully, and I walk back to the ballroom, take my seat on the throne beside Lord Briar, and say,

"Cadmun. Sit." I point at the floor in front of me.

"You know, Dearest One, I am glad you are enjoying your pet, but don't you think he may need to be cleaned up a bit?" Lord Briar says, making a pointed look at Cadmun, with obvious disgust in his eyes.

"You are right, my Lord," I say, turning to Ana, who is dutifully standing behind me as she should be, "Ana, take Cadmun to the baths. Make sure he is clean and dressed properly. Cadmun go with Ana and obey her directions," I command him.

They leave, and I look out at the court, thinking of how one day this will all be mine.

ANA

Apparently, I am just the help now. Yay for me.

"This way, Cadmun," I command. He stands to follow me, and I walk slowly towards the bathing chamber.

My mind wanders as we make our way there. Since I know Cadmun can't wander off, I just let my thoughts flow. What I wouldn't do to take Nix back to her world and pull her out of this world that Lord Stick-Up-His-Butt has placed her in. My beating for not finding the mirror before it broke and for apparently losing Zinn was brutal, as if I could have stopped them from switching places. I am not even sure how that works. My back is still weeping blood, and I can feel it dripping down my spine, making the dress stick to me. I am glad I chose to wear black so it won't show. I am wishing for Nix and Zinn's extra healing mojo right now.

I reach for the door carved in naked Fae and push it open, and find that a few Fae are bathing in the tub. I pay them no mind and take Cadmun to the opposite end of the tub from them.

"Strip," I command Cadmun, and he does. I have to say he is sure easy on the eyes. No wonder Nix fell for him.

May steps up with a tray of bathing supplies, then walks over and scoops up his dirty, travel-worn leathers.

"Oh, May, please get some fresh plain clothes for Cadmun," I say, and she nods and walks away silently.

I see Cadmun with a sad look in his eyes, watching May walk away. I wonder what that is about.

"You in the tub, get cleaned up," I command Cadmun, and he quickly does.

"You know that you probably have known Nix longer than I have," I say to him, and he looks at me questioningly. "Oh, you can't talk, can you?" I realize Nix's glamour still binds him. "You may speak. Tell me all your secrets," I say, releasing Nix's hold on him.

"Thank the Spirits. What do you mean, I have known her longer?" he asks.

"Well, I met her when I was seven, but you knew her before that, didn't you?" I say, thoughtfully.

"Well, maybe it is hard to know. Zinn and Nix switched places so often. But I do remember being very young when I first saw her kyanite-blue eyes, and they drew me in," Cadmun divulges.

"Are you really allowing a human to bathe with us?" A Fae across the tub yells in outrage.

"Looks like it," I say snarkily back.

"Come, let's leave this filth. The tub will have to be drained and cleaned now," the offended Fae announces, and all of the Fae climb out of the tub. They shoot daggers at me, then Cadmun, and exit the bathing chamber.

"Good riddance," I say, and Cadmun looks at me in shock. "What? You think I care what they think? They are all just minions to Lord Stick-Up-His-Butt." Cadmun lets out a small laugh, then covers it with a cough.

"What does that make you?" Cadmun asks sobering up, and now I am questioning my choice to let him speak.

"Well, I am blood oath-bound to him by my family, you idiot. I would break it if I could. You think I like watching from the wings as he is corrupting Nix?" I spit out forcefully.

"Whoa, I do apologize," and he holds up his hands in surrender, and I notice he is holding something in his right hand.

"What is that? Give it to me now!" I command him, and he reaches his hand out to me, and I take the small vial with a drop of iridescent liquid sparkling in it.

"No! Don't take that I need that!" He pleads.

"What is this, and where did you get it? What is your plan?" I demand.

"It is old magic. It is one of Nix's tears from before we came into the Wood. I found it in her pack, which she brought from Bleaker. I was going to slip it into her drink and see if it could save her," he says, then claps his hand over his mouth.

"What did you say? A tear?" I question him again, looking at the vial, and notice it shines a little brighter.

"Yes. I think I can save Nix from what she is becoming with it. Please give it back," he says, genuine desperation in his tone.

"You think this can save her?" I ask again, hoping against all odds that he is right, and I remember Nix's sweet smile.

"Yes," he says desperately.

"Well, if that is true, it is better that I have it than you. I am the one who pours her drinks," I say with a wink, and his jaw drops. "What, do you think I don't want to save her, too? I have seen things I can't unsee. I have stood by far too long. I would do anything to save Nix. I love her."

May enters with fresh clothing and a towel, and we both shut up. This could cost us our lives. May leaves quietly. Cadmun finishes washing, exits the tub, dries, and dresses quickly. When he is sure we are alone, he whispers,

"Then keep it. I trust you to know when the moment is right."

"When the moment is right," I agree.

BRONE

Zinn sings softly about being alone and going home. I breathe the sound in, rather than hear it. Her soft singing breaking something in me. She sings a song I have never heard. Her song ends on a whisper. Her breath evens out, and everything is silent.

I want to speak up and tell her how lovely her voice is, but I hold myself back, knowing it was meant to be a private moment. I can't take any more from her. The snap of the whip sounds in my ears, and a phantom sting lands on my back. Turning, I look at Zinn and see her sleeping soundly, no trace of any pain on her face. I relax and concentrate on how best to get us to the portal opening. The trees will be our best option, no footprints to trace and no scent left to linger on the foliage. With a plan in mind, I find myself falling back asleep.

"Brone. Hey, Brone, wake up. I have to pee," Zinn says, annoyance in her voice.

"Oh. Um… Let me step out," I stutter. I collect my pack and blow out the candle. I let the wet wax fall to the ground, stow it in the bag, and slowly open the roof of our enclosure. I peer out, wait, and listen. Nothing nearby, good.

I create stairs in the earth and climb all the way out and say in a low voice,

"Be quick. We need to get moving. Leave your old dress here so we can hide it in the dirt to block your scent."

"Gotcha," Zinn replies and steps out of view. I take the moment and take care of my own morning needs. As I finish, I see Zinn's black hair poke up out of the enclosure, and she looks around, scanning the area like a predator. My chest swells with pride. She truly is a warrior.

"Come, Zinn. We will travel in the trees. It will be faster and leave a smaller trace for the Seekers who lurk by day. We have Sky running interference for us, but we need to be smart about every move we make," I say seriously.

"Ok, lead the way. I am ready," Zinn replies, bouncing on the balls of her feet.

I turn to assessing the trees and pick a large one with good canopy coverage. The Wood is old, and all the trees merge high up in the canopy. The branches create secret paths for those who know where to find them. Lucky for us, I am one of them. I leap from the ground and push myself up into the tree with the Wind. Zinn follows my example and lands behind me with a smile on her face. My heart stutters at the sight.

"We must talk as little as possible. We must remain hidden. Are you ready? I will be moving fast. Will you be able to keep up?" I ask her.

"Just watch me," she says, a sly smile reaching her lips. Did I put that smile there?

I look at the ground where we have left footprints, and I send a gentle breeze to smooth out the earth. If any Seekers catch my scent and know I have been here, they will know not to follow. I turn and nod at Zinn to signal for her to follow. I turn and run down the long, sturdy branches of the large trees. We weave through the canopy on silent feet. I push myself with the Wind to aid my speed. I find myself continuously looking over my shoulder to make sure that Zinn is behind me. She is always there, keeping pace, never faltering, moving with a grace unlike I've ever seen. We run continuously for hours, and I slow my pace and stop.

"We can rest now," I say.

"I don't need to rest," Zinn complains, but her breath is slightly labored, and I know we both need to drink and eat.

"Come sit with me?" I ask, taking a seat against the body of the large tree we stopped at. I pull out the full waterskin from my pack and hold it out to her. She rolls her eyes, then comes and sits down. Zinn takes the waterskin and drinks deeply.

"Wow, that was great, maybe I did need a break," she admits and wipes her mouth with the back of her hand, drawing my eyes to her lips. I clear my throat and pull out a small cloth-wrapped bundle of berries and nuts and pass it to her. She exchanges the water skin for the food, then opens the bundle and greedily eats it. "How much further until we reach the portal?" she asks, in between bites.

"Maybe half an hour," I tell her, and take a drink of water.

"Brone!" a strong male voice calls from the distance. Zinn and I freeze.

I hold my finger to my lips and gesture for her to come to me. She scoots to me, and I wrap us in the foliage, making us invisible. Through a slit in the leaves, I see a Seeker whose name I don't know searching below us. I hold Zinn a little tighter in what I hope she knows is a signal to stay absolutely still. She remains frozen in my arms. I am at a loss as to how he tracked us. How could he trace us in the trees? I loosen my grip on Zinn, preparing myself to fight, but a flurry of motion to the right catches my eye. Making my heart race. I am such a fool. Of course, things wouldn't be this easy.

"Over here, you brute!" I hear Sky shout and watch as the old Fae simultaneously knocks the Seeker down with a gust of Wind, then binds him so tight with vines that the Seeker's face turns purple. I watch as Sky bends down and punches the Seeker hard in the face, knocking him out,

"Coast is clear, you two better run!" Sky calls out and disappears in the direction he came from.

"I got you," I say, releasing the foliage, pulling Zinn into my arms, and taking off at my full speed.

I run effortlessly along the tangle of branches and don't stop or slow until the branches become increasingly less dense as we reach the edge of the Wood. I jump down, carefully placing Zinn on the ground.

"You know I won't break, right?" She asks teasingly, rewarding me with another small smile.

"I know you won't," I say, my words weighted with meaning, "Come, we travel on foot from here." I take Zinn's hand and walk the remaining distance to the large ring of clover that will take her to the other realm.

"There, you see the clover ring?" I ask her, point to it, release her hand, and feel the loss of contact acutely.

"You mean that circle of clover can take me back to Nix's realm?" She questions, looking unconvinced.

"Yes," is all I reply.

"I just stand in it? Is that easy?" She asks in disbelief.

"Yes, it is that easy," I say, the finality of the situation setting in. She will go, and I must stay.

She begins walking toward the circle and hesitates. She turns and says,

"Thank… Watch out!" Zinn shouts, then she reaches and snatches two daggers from her thighs, and they whip by my head on either side, missing by inches as they pass. I whip around to watch them embed into the oncoming Fae's chest. He falls dead. She runs to his now still body, frees her blades, wipes them in the grass, and returns them to their sheaths. She opens the earth, and it swallows the body whole, leaving no trace that the Fae was ever even there. I am proud and terrified by her deadly accuracy at the same time. Zinn had no fear, no hesitation, just clean action. She runs to me, grabs my hand, and says,

"Come on."

Then she pulls us both into the ring of clover, and the world tilts on its axis when it rights itself again. We are in an open circular clearing somewhere in Nix's world.

DANIEL

"Young man, are you paying attention? Do you understand what I am telling you?" Doctor Fraund questions me.

"You think I am crazy," I say flatly.

"I am not saying that. I am saying we need to hold you for an evaluation. It is called 5150. You will be held here for observation for seventy-two hours, and we can go from there," he replies calmly as if I were a child.

"You should remember, Nix. You treated her, her whole life!" I shout.

"I see. This girl you keep talking about, Nix, when did you first meet her?" he asks, writing down notes.

"When we were three. We were best friends. Then she broke my arm. Look, I still have the scar from where they had to put the pins in my arm," I say, and show him my arm, but I am shocked when I no longer have the scar.

"I see no scar. Do you?" He asks, looking concerned, as he writes notes on his notepad.

"Well, no, but I swear it was there," I say, rubbing where the scar used to be.

Frustration makes me bang my fists on the table, denting the surface, and a ringing starts in my ears, causing me to grab the sides of my head and double over. Dr. Fraund stands, backing away, signaling an orderly into the room. I stand, pacing back and forth, and the ringing in my ears does not stop. It increases. I am suddenly restrained, and a needle is pushed into my arm. I pass out.

NIX

I am out in the courtyard, working on my magic. I have learned more control than I have ever known. I can now convert water into ice and then instantly evaporate it. I don't feel the old drain I used to in my human form. I am toying with vines, winding them in my fingers in intricate knots, when Lord Briar's voice startles me,

"You are most talented, Dearest One."

"It is thanks to you for showing me," I reply shyly.

"Don't be so modest, it isn't becoming for someone of your station," he instructs.

"Thank… I will keep that in mind," I say, almost thanking him, and he cuts me a sharp glance due to my slip-up.

"You have practiced enough for one day. You may spend the rest of the morning doing whatever you wish. Then come to the throne room," he commands, more than tells me.

"Yes, my Lord," I reply, and I keep some of the vines on my arms as decoration and a sign of my power.

I walk towards the doors, reaching the spot I instructed Cadmun to sit at, "Come now, Cadmun," I command, and he follows me as I wander the halls.

I am not sure what to do with myself. I wander into the antechamber and stop to admire the ceiling. I have learned that the image depicts the infamous twins Aurora and Poe, who almost destroyed not just this realm but also my old one as well. Their actions fractured the walls that separated the realms, making this world open to human entry. That was their mistake. They brought the lesser beings into this realm. Lord Briar's ancestors finally brought down the twins. I consider how the twins' actions ultimately led to Verna's final betrayal, causing Thorne to curse the land. Without the twins' mistake, the balance would have remained. I turn to Cadmun and wonder what he may think of this. So I release my binding on him and ask,

"Do you know the story of the twins?" Then add, " You may speak."

"No, and I don't care to," he replies curtly.

"That is a shame. I thought you liked knowing everything," I say, thinking of Jameson's library.

"I don't care to learn anything about these creatures that you are so fond of now you forget your humanity," he says, glaring at me.

"Why should I remember it?" I ask, watching the alarm light in his eyes, and it makes me smile. "Come, Cadmun," I command.

"You know you don't have to glamour me. I would always follow you, Little Flower," Cadmun says softly, and I am taken aback by his nickname for me coming out of his mouth.

We enter the ballroom. I watch as the crowd parts for me like I am something to be feared, and I relish it. I make it to the throne and take my seat beside Lord Briar. I look at Cadmun and command him to sit. I have had a pillow laid out by my feet for him to occupy while I am here.

"Here, I got this for you," Ana says, handing me a glass of wine, a strange look passing between her and Cadmun. I nod at her and take a sip, and feel a strange prickling sensation.

"You know I still don't believe you are who you are pretending to be. I know your humanity remains," Cadmun says low but loud enough for those close to the throne to hear, and most importantly, Lord Briar. Small gasps echo in the room.

"You forget your place, human," Lord Briar says, steel in his voice.

"I didn't remember to have him stay quiet," I say, realizing my mistake.

"Now you must be punished, pet. Nix drain him. Humans do not question our ways and get away with it," Lord Briar demands.

I take another sip of wine. I feel a sharp pain in my heart afterward. I clear my throat, shaking the feeling off.

"Yes, my Lord," I say and raise my hand and direct it toward Cadmun. As I begin to drain him, I feel the rush flow into me, but it isn't quite right. His body bows back, and suddenly, I remember our kiss, and the euphoria that usually hits me is replaced by a bittersweet feeling that leaves a bad taste in my mouth. I falter and break the connection.

"What is the meaning of this?" Lord Briar demands.

"He is so divine. I think I will save the rest for later, my Lord," I lie, trying to cover my inability to continue draining Cadmun.

"I see you choose the cake," Lord Briar says, smiling devilishly at me.

ZINN

I stumble a few steps, and I realize we are in the clearing behind the elementary school. I realize as I look around, I don't belong in this world. It feels like an alien planet. I take in our surroundings and gasp and cover my mouth as I see two withered corpses nearby. What happened here? Brone tracks my line of sight, and they land on the bodies.

"What do you think happened?" I ask Brone, and I approach the bodies.

"I am not sure, but it is clear they are Fae. Look at their ears." He says, inspecting them, then bends down to inspect them more closely and pulls something from the smaller body's hand—white hair.

"Nix," I whisper, not wanting to believe she would ever be involved in something so horrific.

"Yes, it looks like she was involved with this," Brone says solemnly, standing and coming to my side.

"We can't leave them here like this," I tell him.

Reaching out, I extend my hand and let their bodies slowly sink into the earth. As I close the earth over them, I will a little more magic out, making small, stars of the Wood flowers bloom over their makeshift grave. I feel Brone place his hand gently on my shoulder, and he says,

"They are beautiful."

"Let's get going," I reply, my focus returning to the reason we are here in the first place, Daniel.

"I do not know this world here. I must follow," Brone says in his slight annoyance in his gravelly voice.

"What? You don't like to follow?" I ask in a teasing tone.

"I have followed for too long, but I will follow you," he says, and I catch him looking at me with something like longing. Maybe?

"We can't use magic in this realm, out in the open. If someone saw, we would bring too much attention to ourselves," I say to Brone with a warning look. "Let's go. Follow me," I tell him, and we walk toward the small trail that will lead us out of the forest clearing. Once we make it to the playground, I pick up my pace and head towards Daniel's house. It feels so strange to be in Hawthorn again. The perfect houses and lawns no longer seem as appealing as they once did.

It feels like a dream. Not only am I in Hawthorn, but I am also on my way to see Daniel in my own body. We make our way through the neighborhood until we find ourselves standing in front of Daniel's house. His black Subaru was parked in the driveway. Now that I am here, I have a weird feeling I can't describe.

"Maybe you should wait here," I say to Brone, not knowing how Daniel will react to my new appearance. A nonhuman appearance thanks to Nix.

"No. Where you go, I go. If we need to, we can glamour anyone in there to forget we were ever here," Brone says, leaving no room for argument in his tone.

"Fine," I concede, since I do not know how to glamour anyone.

I walk to the door and open it, not knowing what I will find. As I walk in, I hear a woman crying softly in the dining room. I hold up my finger, signaling for Brone to stay quiet. He nods, showing he understands. We creep up the stairs to Daniel's room. I crack open the door. I step inside, and the room is empty. No one is here. I don't understand. Daniel's car is outside, so he must be here. The sounds of a woman's voice comes from the direction of the stairs. So, I quietly close the door, realizing it must be Daniel's mom.

"I don't know what to do," I hear her say, pressing my ear against the door to hear better. "I don't know what is happening. He has never had a problem like this before, Dr. Fraund," I hear her say.

That name gives me a flashback to another time. Now I am really straining to listen.

"He is being violent?" She questions, "He is claiming some girl named Nix exists and is missing? Who is she? I have never heard of her," Daniel's mom says, and my hand flies up to my mouth. They're talking about Nix, well, maybe me.

"How much longer does he have to be in the hospital?" Daniel's mom asks.

My heart implodes. Is Daniel in the hospital? What has happened? Why doesn't his mom recognize my name? I broke Daniel's arm when we were little. She should definitely know who I am. What is going on?

"Another day? It has already been two. Isn't he improving? What do you mean, he might have to stay longer? Ok. Yes. Ok. Please help him. Thank you, Doctor, yes, ok. Bye," Daniel's mom says. I hear footsteps pass. A door opens, then closes, and then soft crying starts.

"Ok. Something isn't right here," I whisper and turn to Brone, who is holding a small, black thing. When he sees me looking, he pockets it quickly.

"I think Daniel is being held at the hospital, and for some reason, no one knows who I am. Ok, well, Nix, but I was here. Oh, you know what, it doesn't matter. We need to go there immediately. But we need a disguise. We can't walk across town looking like goth enforcers in our leathers. We also need to hide our ears," I am saying to myself more than I am to Brone.

I walk over to Daniel's closet and pull out two oversized hoodies. I throw one at Brone and say,

"Put that on."

I move to the dresser, searching through the drawers, and score when I find one full of sweats. I pull out two pairs. I toss one pair of pants to Brone, and he catches them deftly. We quickly pull the clothes on over our leathers. I can't help but smirk at how funny Brone looks in modern clothing.

"Ok, pull up your hood," I say as I tie my sweats as tight as they can go, then roll the waistband a few times so I am not drowning in them.

"Let's go out through the window. No one will see us use magic to get down," I say, pushing past Brone, pulling up my own hood.

I open the window, check that no one is around, jump, and use a current of air to slow my fall. Brone follows my lead, and we walk toward the hospital and, hopefully, toward Daniel.

ANA

Nix has arrived in the ballroom and takes her seat on her throne next to Lord Stick-Up-His-Butt. I turn my back on the court and pour Nix her usual glass of wine. I pull the small vial from my sleeve, then let the precious glowing tear drop into the red liquid.

"Here, I got this for you," I say, handing the tear-laced wine to Nix. I meet Cadmun's eyes. He gives me a tiny nod, knowing I have done my part. Nix takes a sip. She slightly twitches.

"You know I still don't believe you are who you are pretending to be. I know your humanity remains," Cadmun says low but loud enough for those close to the throne to hear, and most importantly, Lord Stick-Up-His-Butt. Small gasps echo in the room.

"You forget your place, human," Lord Stick-Up-His-Butt says, steel in his voice.

"I didn't remember to have him stay quiet," Nix says, keeping her features neutral, but I notice her place her hand to her chest.

"Now you must be punished, pet. Nix drain him. Humans do not question our ways and get away with it," Lord Stick-Up-His-Butt demands.

Oh my god. It didn't work. Nix takes another large drink of the wine and places it on the table next to her. I see her wince noticeably. The smallest amount of hope sparks in me that the tear did, in fact, do something.

"Yes, Lord Briar," Nix says and extends her hand toward Cadmun. His body arches, and she begins pulling the Spirit from him. Shit, it didn't work, and she is going to kill him. Suddenly, she falters and breaks the hold on Cadmun, and relief floods me.

"What is the meaning of this?" Briar directs towards Nix.

"He is so divine. I think I will save the rest for later, my Lord," Nix replies sweetly, washing away any hope I had for saving her.

"I see you choose the cake," Lord Stick-Up-His-Butt says, sickening me by whatever he means by cake.

I have to keep my shit together and not run to Cadmun. I don't know him all that well, but I know he wants to save Nix just as badly as I do. Will he still want to now, though? I am not so sure. Nix is staring down at him. He is passed out on the ground at her feet, and she looks slightly lost. Then she shakes her head slightly.

"Ana," Nix says, turning to me. I quickly try to look calm.

"Yeah," I reply casually, which earns me a look from Lord Stick-Up-His-Butt.

"See that Cadmun is taken to my chambers. I do not wish to look at him," she says coolly, but her hands are slightly trembling.

"Oh, uh, ok," I say, looking around for Brone.

Then I realize I haven't seen him since Zinn's disappearance. Where could he be? Is he still searching for Zinn? Isn't he supposed to be like the best Seeker of all time or something? Well, shit. How am I supposed to move him? Then I spot the human enslaved walking around serving drinks to the rowdy Fae. I spot May and signal for her to come, and she slowly approaches the throne.

"May, can you have two strong men remove Nix's, um, pet to her quarters right away?" I ask her, and May scurries away and does as I ask.

Two strong men come and carry Cadmun away. I am so disappointed. How could Nix do this? And to Cadmun? I thought she loved him once. Has her heart hardened that much? The tear must not have worked, damn it. I look one last time at Cadmun's limp body being carried from the room, and I feel sick.

"My Lord, I think I may have had too much to drink. I think I will go to my chambers," Nix says to Briar.

He nods, and she stands to leave.

"Ana, will you walk with me? I feel a bit dizzy," she asks me, and I walk over, and she links her arm in mine, her balance a little off. She didn't have that much to drink. I don't know what is going on with her.

We walk slowly to her chambers, and she whispers,

"Do you think he is ok?"

Oh shit! Maybe the tear did do something after all. I don't allow myself to feel too much hope. Maybe I should press her a little.

"Why? Do you suddenly care?" I ask harshly before I can stop myself.

She jerks slightly and asks,

"What do you mean by that?"

"Well, you don't seem to care about him. You are treating him more like an animal than a person." I quip, pushing her buttons.

"Well, how do you expect me to treat him?" She asks, coldness creeping into her voice once more.

Shit. Maybe I pushed too hard.

"Well, don't you love him? Not too long ago, you were concerned about his well-being, and you just almost drained him completely," I say, gentling my tone slightly.

"Love him? I am not so sure. I thought I did," she says softly, honesty in her voice, and she slightly leans into me, my heart jumps at her old response to being upset.

The tone in her voice reminded me of my old friend, the Nix I used to know. We reach her chambers, and she reaches for the knob and says, "Even if it isn't love, I still do care. I think?" She says, a question in her voice.

DANIEL

I wake to the smell of hospital disinfectant. I open my eyes slowly and look around. They brought me back to my room. I stand and head to the sink and splash water on my face to wake myself up. The cuts on my cheek, stinging from the water, bring my mind into focus once more. The curtain that acts as a door to my room opens, and Dr. Fraund steps in.

"I see you are awake," he says in a cold voice.

"Looks like it," I reply flatly.

"Tell me how you are feeling. Do you still think that this Nix is missing?" He asks, lifting a clipboard to write down my answer.

No matter what I say or do, this man doesn't seem to get that I am not lying. So, I stay silent.

"You know silence speaks louder than words sometimes. You should join the others in the group activities then," he instructs and turns to leave me.

Frustrated, I slam my fists down on the sink, and it breaks off the wall, water shooting everywhere. The painful ringing in my ears begins. I stumble.

"We need sedation in here!" Dr. Fraund yells.

An orderly enters with a syringe in his meaty hand. I fight this time, pushing him off of me with a strength that is not my own. He hits the wall across my room and crumbles to the ground.

"Help! I need more help in here!" Dr. Fraund yells, backing away from me, fear in his eyes.

The ringing in my ears reaches the point that it sounds like an alarm is beating against my eardrums. I try to cover my ears to stop the sound. As I cover them, I feel liquid dripping out of them. I move my hands to see what it is, and there is blood. What is happening? Fear grips me, and I fall to my knees, too weak to stand. Someone grabs me from behind. I feel the pinch of a needle in my neck, and once again, I am unconscious.

BRONE

I keep up with Zinn's quick pace as we walk, wishing we could just use the wind to push us. I follow her through this strange world. I have only been here once before, when I brought her to my world. She keeps her head down, and we pass humans giving us curious glances.

"Don't look so shocked. You look awkward. You need to look more casual and not so… well, so Brone-like," Zinn says, flustered.

"I don't know what you mean," I say, confused by what she is saying.

"Just look, you know casual, relaxed, cool," she says, looking at me with her sly smile.

"It is hard to be cool in these clothes," I say, pulling at the collar of the strange half-cloak she gave me.

"Well, sorry about that. We didn't have that many options that would fit over our leathers. It is hot, isn't it?" she says, fanning her face a bit. "We're almost there—just two more blocks. Turn here," she says, and we take a left.

"You seem to know this land very well," I compliment her.

"Well, I should. I have had to come here most of my childhood," she says, sadness touching her eyes.

I am not sure what I have done to upset her, so I keep my mouth shut as we approach a large rectangular building that says 'Hawthorn Psychiatric Hospital'. What a strange place this is. It smells cold and has a pungent odor that wafts all the way outside. Zinn takes a steadying breath, looks at me, and says,

"Here goes nothing."

We enter through doors that magically open on their own, and she heads to a large desk, where a blonde-haired human woman sits.

"Excuse me, but do you have a patient named Daniel McCallister here?" Zinn asks the blonde woman.

The woman looks at Zinn with a strange face. Then does a double-take when she sees me. I squirm under her gaze and check my hood to be sure my ears haven't become exposed. The blonde turns her face back to Zinn and says,

"Sorry, but I can't give out any information about patients that may or may not be here."

Zinn starts fidgeting, looks at me, and nods her head toward the blonde. I shrug my shoulders and give her a puzzled look. She clears her throat and nods at the woman again, and I am still lost.

"Oh, for Spirit's sake, glamour her and have her tell us already," she says, flustered.

Realization sinks in, and I feel like a fool. I forgot she was never taught the skill.

"Tell us what we want to know," I command the blonde.

Her eyes turn glassy, and she says,

"Yes, he is here."

"Where?" Zinn asks desperately.

"Unit two is currently under lockdown. A patient had a meltdown," the blonde says.

"What do you mean?" Zinn asks impatiently.

"There was an incident, and now it is locked down. Only people with pass keys can enter the unit," the blonde replies, looking confused.

"Well, take us," Zinn says in a clearly frustrated tone.

"I don't have one," the blonde says.

"Shit," Zinn says under her breath, then continues with, "Who does and where can we find them?"

"The orderlies, nurses, and doctors all have one," the blonde says, obviously getting distressed by this line of questioning.

"Where the hell do I find one of them?" Zinn demands pounding the counter with a fist.

"Someone should be in the break room. It is down the hallway to the right, past the bathrooms," the blonde says and covers her mouth as if it will keep her from talking.

Zinn starts stalking in the direction the blonde just told us, and I say,

"Stay here. Alert no one to our presence."

I pick up my pace and follow Zinn. She heads into what I assume is the 'break room', then turns and signals me to hurry up, so I start to jog toward her. When I enter the doorway, three humans are staring at Zinn: two women in matching light green outfits and a thin man in a white coat.

"That one, Zinn says and points to the man," anger filling her eyes most exquisitely.

"You two stay," I command the women, "You come with us and keep your mouth shut, and follow our instructions," I command the male.

"Lead us to unit two," Zinn says, "Remember me, Doctor Fraund?"

The man shakes his head, no recognition in his eyes.

"Oh, I guess you wouldn't, would you? Do you remember Nix? I mean, how could you forget harming a child, unless that is something you do to all children? The things you did to us to try to cure us of a problem that actually didn't exist. Your day will come, doctor. You are lucky I have better things to do than waste time on your sorry ass, or I would kick the shit out of you right here, right now," Zinn says, vengeance in her eyes.

The man looks terrified. I almost expect him to wet his britches. We follow him through the white hallways. He stops at a door with a black box attached, then stands there.

"Well, open it," Zinn says, pointing at the black box, and the sweet pheromones of glamour slip from her mouth.

The man does as she instructs, and he does as she says. He holds a card attached to a string in his pocket and goes to the box. He holds the card to the box, and the door buzzes, startling me; then it opens.

"Give that to me, and stay here," Zinn commands, and he hands her the card. She swings back her arm and lands a punch right in the center of his face. The man gasps, grabs his nose, and falls to his knees.

"That is for Nix," Zinn says and walks through the open door.

"What was that about?" I question Zinn, and she replies,

"It is a long story. Let's just say he isn't a very nice man." She says, curtly.

We enter another short hallway that opens into a room with tables and chairs, where a few humans in plain gray matching outfits mill about.

"Tell them to stay put," Zinn says, and she heads toward a room with curtains separating it from the larger main room.

"All of you stay where you are," I command the small group of humans.

She pulls the curtain aside, then turns to me and says,

"Check the other rooms, on that side, while I check these."

"What am I looking for?" I ask because I don't know.

"A young human with short, messy brown hair and topaz eyes," Zinn tells me, anxiety laces her words.

Zinn rushes to the next room, pulls the curtain back, and turns away from it, while I hurry to the other side of the room. We both check all the rooms but find them all vacant.

"Shit. Where is he?" Zinn says to herself more than she says to me.

"Doctor Fraund? What happened? What is going on?" a voice from the hallway sounds.

A large, scruffy-looking human dressed in all white hurries into the room.

"Hey! You can't be in here!" he yells at us and starts rushing towards Zinn.

"Freeze," I say stopping him in his tracks and pull vines through the hard floor to secure him.

"Where is he?" Zinn's voice echoes off the walls, the room filling with the sweet aroma that only glamour can bring.

I stand there stunned by how powerful she is.

"Who?" the scruffy human says.

"Daniel. Where is Daniel?" Zinn says with slight desperation in her voice.

"We had to put him in isolation, please don't hurt me," the man pleads.

"Where is isolation? Answer me now," Zinn commands.

"Through that door," he says and nods to the only other solid door in the entire room.

The room also has a black box on it. Zinn rushes to it, and the man shouts,

"Hey, you can't go in there, he is dangerous!"

Zinn fumbles with the card and holds it to the black box until the same buzzing sound comes, and then the door clicks open.

I rush to her, not knowing what will be in there, and I see him. The boy she has been trying to save this whole time, strapped down by his hands and ankles to a bed. Unconscious.

Zinn rushes in and begins to try to undo the leather straps with shaking hands, but can't seem to get them off. I hurry to her side, distress on her face. I place a steadying hand on hers and say,

"Let me."

NIX

I open the door to my chambers and see Cadmun lying on my bed. I slowly approach him and see that he is paler than usual but is breathing deeply. His breath calms the strange tug on my heart that I have felt since I thought of our kiss. I sit next to him and run my fingers through his thick black hair. His eyes slightly flutter, and I pull my hand back. He opens his eyes, and I feel like he is looking into my soul.

"Why," he says in a whisper.

"I don't know anymore. It felt like the right thing, but then it didn't," I tell him honestly.

"You stopped," he says, his voice a little stronger.

"Yes, I couldn't do it. Not to you. I will not lose you, Cadmun," I hear the truth ringing in my words.

"You could never lose me, Little Flower. I know you are in there. I see you. Come back to me," he says, reaching up to touch my face, and I turn into it.

Feeling his soft touch reminds me of something I have been missing since I first arrived at the Great Tree. Closeness. Warmth. Love? I want to feel close, so I lie down next to him and nuzzle my face into the crook of his neck. He turns his head and breathes in deeply and presses a soft kiss to the top of my head. Before I can stop, I turn my face to him and brush my lips, feather soft, against his.

"I knew it would work," he says softly against my mouth.

"What would work?" I ask, becoming breathless at the thought of kissing him deeper.

"The tear. The tear worked. Are you really back, Little Flower?" Cadmun asks softly.

"What do you mean, tear?" I ask, puzzled, pulling away slightly.

"You know the tear I took from you long ago. The tear from your bag," he replies, and tries to bring me close again.

Realization hits me—the wine. Then anger hits me.

Ana.

ZINN

I watch as Brone breaks the restraints from the table one by one. Daniel stirs, and I whisper,

"I am here now."

"Nix?" Daniel whispers, and I freeze.

Brone looks me in the eyes, and I can't hide my pain. I take a step back and watch as Brone lifts Daniel from the table.

"What now?" Brone asks, and I realize I didn't really think this through.

"Well, I am not sure. I don't really even understand why he is here," I say, and know exactly who I need to talk to.

"Follow me," I say, and head back to the door of the unit.

"Forget all of this," Brone says, and it echoes through the unit.

He pulls the vines from the orderly, and they recede into the floor, and the floor looks perfect again. Then I see my target. Still clutching his nose, I say,

"Have him tell us why Daniel is here," I bite out harshly at Brone, realizing my anger at myself is coming out. I need to get my shit together.

"I think you will find you can get the information yourself," Brone says in a knowing voice I don't understand, then nods toward Doctor Fraund. Realization hits me, and I understand. Concentrating on what I want, I look at this simpering man and command,

"Why is he here?"

"Well, you see, he is having a delusion that a girl has gone missing, well, two girls, but he is fixated on one named Nix. But the girls he keeps talking about don't exist."

"What are you talking about?" I say, getting flustered, and I hear Daniel groan.

"Well, as I said, this—Nix she doesn't exist. He has been violent as well. He destroyed property at Hawkes. When he came here, he had more violent tendencies as well. He knocked the entire sink off the wall in his room just today. He should not be out in public, given his delusions and violent behavior. He is dangerous," Doctor Fraund warns.

"They must have glamoured the whole town, Zinn," Brone says, stepping closer, "and I think your friend is waking up," he finishes.

I look over to see Daniel stirring in Brone's strong arms.

"Here, set him down on the couch," I ask Brone, directing him to the rundown piece of furniture.

Brone places Daniel down with care and steps back. I move to Daniel's side and kneel on the floor. Daniels' eyes flutter open, and his topaz eyes lock on me.

"I knew it. I knew you were real," he says, his voice full of relief.

"Yes, I am real," I reply, unable to tell the whole truth.

I glance at Brone and ever so slightly shake my head no, and I hope he understands my signal. Daniel's hand reaches up and pulls back my hood, and the soft look in his eyes is replaced by shock. I realize he must have seen my ears and panic bubbles in my gut.

"What are you?" Daniel says, scrambling into a sitting position.

"It's me. It's me Zi… Nix," I say, trying to calm him, but his eyes grow wild.

"Who are you really? What are you?" Daniel questions, stands, stumbles a little, then starts backing away.

"Ok, my name is Zinn," I start to explain.

"Zinn? I thought you were a dream," Daniel says, shaking his head. "No, no, no, this isn't right. You're a dream. This isn't real."

Daniel grabs the sides of his head and starts mumbling to himself.

"I can help you. I swear, trust me, I am real. It's me, Zinn, you just always knew me as Nix. It is hard to explain, but this is real. Remember your dreams? We met on a beach. Don't you remember…"

"Stop!" Daniel shouts and throws his hands up in the air, and a strong gust of Wind suddenly throws me down.

"Uhhh… Not again," Daniel says, grabbing the sides of his head.

"He has magic," Brone says and rushes to stand between us in a fighting stance.

Daniel falls to his knees, his palms land in front of him, and vines begin to break through the floor and creep up his arms.

"No, Brone. Stop!" I shout.

"That isn't me," Brone replies, and he looks down at me.

"Then who is it?" I ask, frantically looking around for any other threats, but there is just Daniel.

Daniel starts hyperventilating, and the vines start to encase his body.

"Daniel, please, it's ok, it's me!" I plead, "Brone, help? What do we do?" I ask frantically.

"He needs to calm down," Brone says with urgency in his voice.

Ok, calm, but how?

"Zinn, the vines are going to kill him," Brone warns.

The vines are circling Daniel's neck, and I am so scared and try to think of how to stop him from hurting himself. I do the only thing that I can think of, and I start singing 'Young and Beautiful' by Lana Del Rey.

DANIEL

Vines creep up my body, constricting my movement. They begin to wrap around my throat, and it is hard to breathe. The ringing in my ears is the worst it has ever been. But then I hear it. Her voice. Her sweet voice fills me. I focus on the sound, and I begin to relax. The vines begin to loosen and trail back to the floor, falling limp. I breathe for the first time in weeks. I look toward the girl with pointed ears and finally see her. Those smoky gray eyes stare at me. I would know those eyes anywhere, and I know it is real. It is her. Zinn. The girl from the beach, from my dreams.

ANA

I am standing behind the throne, wondering when this nightmare of a night will end. Without Nix here, I am just part of the background. No one approaches me. I am not welcome here. I miss my time in Nix's world. I miss her. My mind spirals for a moment, and I wonder where Zinn is in all of this? I stop that train at the station, but it pulls right up to the moment Nix stopped draining Cadmun. Why did she stop? I asked her if she loved him. She seemed so confused by that. I allow myself to hope. If Nix was too far gone, would she even have given love a second thought? Maybe the tear did the trick. I saw a tiny piece of Nix. My Nix.

The door to the ballroom bangs open with a strong gust of Wind, and some revelers are knocked to the floor. Lord Briar stands ready to fight. Then I see her. Nix. Rage simmers in her cold blue eyes. Oh shit, she drained him. Power is swirling around her. She has her new ornamental vines decorating her arms, which slither in snake-like patterns, almost seeming alive. Lord Briar realizes it is her and reclaims his seat, but his eyes are intent on her. Nix approaches the throne and stops.

"You!" she says, and I know she knows.

"Me," I say flatly, hiding my fear.

"What did you do to me?" She says, a threat laced in her voice.

"What is this? What has Ana done now, Dearest One?" Lord Stick-Up-His-Butt asks quizzically.

"That traitorous bitch tried to poison me," Nix spits and points at me.

Lord Stick-Up-His-Butt rises from his throne and turns to face me. Oh shit, I am really done for now. I don't care, though it was worth it. If I die tonight, at least I know I tried.

"Poison? You tried to poison your princess?" Briar says, giving me a loaded look.

"It wasn't poison, Nix, you idiot," I say, not caring about the consequences.

"What do you call spiking my drink with magic?" Nix fires back.

"I was trying to save you from this evil Bastard!" I say and point my finger at Lord Stick-Up-His-Butt.

Gasps ring out amongst the crowd. I have really done it now. I know this will be my last night on this earth. I feel vines shoot up from the ground and bind my arms and pull me to my knees.

"You will be made to kneel before me, Ana. Your mouth has finally gone too far," Briar proclaims, "You will be severely punished for what you have done to my Dearest One and that mouth of yours."

"If I thought it would work, I would do it again, but apparently, you are too far gone. You don't even know how to love anymore," I call to Nix. "I don't even know who you have become. But this," I say, pointing my chin toward her, "This is what you are now. Who you are now isn't the girl I love. The girl who was my friend."

Nix comes to stand by her father. Her vines slither down from her arms and come toward me,

"Let me take care of that smart mouth," she says, and the vines wrap around my mouth, gagging me.

Lord Briar raises his hand in my direction, and I brace for what is to come. Nix places her hand on his arm gently, and he looks at her with a question in his eyes.

"Let me, my Lord," she says calmly and steps forward, raising her palm to face me.

I plead with my eyes to Nix, but nothing looks back. Just an empty void of blue. I jerk in my binds, but I am caught like a rat in a trap. Then it begins. I feel a sharp, invasive power invade my body, and I feel it tug on my soul. It burns as bright as the sun, burning me alive from the inside. Her power sinks its claws into me and utterly shreds me apart. It invades my body, pulling the very essence of my being along with it. I can't breathe. My sight is darkening, and

I know this is the end of me. My body feels as if it's about to cave in on itself, and I scream through my gag.

"No, Dearest One, that is enough," Lord Briar says in a commanding tone, and the pull keeps its hold on me. "I said enough!" he shouts, and the pull releases me, and I collapse.

How? How could she do it? The vines retreat from my mouth and return to Nix's arms. I say breathlessly,

"I thought you were my friend. I know you. This isn't you."

"You're wrong, you see, I never even existed," Nix says and turns her back on me.

Tears sting my eyes, and I realize she is right. She never existed.

ZINN

Daniel looks into my eyes, and I see the spark of recognition. The vines fall from his body. He stands on wobbly legs. I see blood coming from his nose and ears, and fear spikes in me. I rush to him, but I stop short, not wanting to freak him out, and I ask desperately,

"Are you ok?"

"Zinn?" he whispers.

The sound of my name on his lips frees something heavy that I have been carrying my whole life. I slowly approach. I am not sure how he will react. Something strange has happened. The magic that flows from him isn't normal. The magic radiates off him like static electricity.

"Be careful," Brone says, blocking me with a protective arm, stopping my approach.

"No, I've got this," I say and move his arm from my path.

Daniel stands, never breaking eye contact, watches me approach, then takes the smallest step back. I stop, and he asks,

"Is this real?"

"Yes," I say and move forward, gauging his reaction, his face full of confusion.

He closes the distance between us in two swift steps and wraps his arms around me. A rush of relief floods me, and yet it feels slightly off. His arms around me do not make me feel like they did a few weeks ago, and I am confused, but I think of what Sky said about the necklace. He said it takes what we want the most but brings it to us in the worst way, or some riddle like that. I feel doubt for the first time, and I don't know what any of it means.

"I knew you were real," Daniel says softly into my ear, and I shiver.

"Careful, Zinn," Brone says in a warning tone and steps toward us.

Daniel's eyes fly open, and he yells,

"Stop!"

Wind so strong surges from him that both Brone and I are knocked to the ground. Daniel falls to his knees immediately and grabs his head. Brone quickly recovers, and I scramble over to Daniel.

"What is happening to me?" Daniel moans and passes out again, fresh blood running slowly from his nose.

"He has strong magic, but how?" Brone says, leaning over us. Daniel is going in and out of consciousness. The realization hits me like a freight train—the mirror. Where is it?

"Daniel, did you find my box in your car?" I question, shaking him gently, but I need answers fast.

"Yes," he says, focus coming back in his eyes, and he spots Brone over my shoulder, and fear sparks in his eyes.

"Don't be afraid of him. Focus. Focus on me, Daniel," I softly turn his face, which has cuts on it, toward me and ask, "Did you open it?"

"I did. I broke your mirror. I am so sorry, Zinn. I saw you in the mirror, and I dropped it, and the mirror shattered, but someone took it," Daniel says in a rush of urgent words.

"Brone, I think that he absorbed the power locked in the mirror," I say, and the pieces fall into place.

Briar wanting. No need for the mirror. To fully power Nix and push her over the edge. He wants her to be the most powerful Fae in the whole realm. This is his endgame. With her under his power, he could even come to this realm and take control of the entire human world with Nix as his weapon. Dread fills me, and I look at Brone.

"What? What is it?" Brone asks with urgency.

"I think the magic that was trapped in the mirror transferred to Daniel. I don't know how, but that must be it," I reason out loud, "Nix pulled the magic stored in the mirror in our world before she went to the Wood. It was so much magic, Cadmun even felt it from miles away from Bleaker."

Brone's eyes fill with understanding.

"You must take it from the boy," Brone says with finality.

"How? What if I hurt him? I don't even know how to do Spirit magic. I only know what it feels like when it is taken and I can't, no, I won't do that to him," I say with resolve.

"Zinn, please make it stop," Daniel says, voice getting stronger.

Alarms sound, and shouts come from the hallway.

"Times up. We have to go," Brone says and helps Daniel to his feet, and pulls one of Daniel's arms over his shoulder. Brone points his hand toward the vines Daniel created with his wild magic, and they recede into the ground. The floor seals, and there is no trace of them ever being there.

"Where? Where do we go?" I ask desperately, jumping up, ready to run.

"Back to the portal. We need Sky. He will know what to do," Brone says, and I take Daniel's other arm, and we rush from the hospital as fast as we can. Orderlies rush at us, and Brone commands,

"Stop! Forget us once we are gone."

The orderlies freeze, and a glassy look washes over their eyes, and we hurry from the building, alarms still screaming.

ANA

The ground is cold and hard beneath me. I am so weak. I open my eyes with effort and see I am in Zinn's cage. I sit up too fast, and my head starts swimming. I might puke. I push myself into a sitting position. I thought it worked, but she drained me. How? How could she do it? My mind hears her voice:

"I never existed."

Zinn, it was her all along. The girl who sings snorted when she laughed, and the one I betrayed. I stood by and watched while my friend was beaten and drained, and I did nothing. Tears run down my cheeks, my chest tightens, and I sob into my hands. The door opens, and I watch as Briar strides in with a satisfied smirk.

"Look how far you have fallen. How does it feel? You watched your true friend be tortured. You tried to change Nix when she didn't want to be changed. Now you will sit in here and rot. Oh, it will be so sweet to watch you see your friends' true demise."

"What do you mean, demise?" I ask, and it feels like ice is creeping under my skin.

"I must say, I thought you would have puzzled it out for yourself by now," he says, pure evil in his eyes.

"Puzzled what out? What are you talking about?" I ask, with confusion mixed with dread.

"Well, they both will die, of course. You didn't really think I would let a half-breed rule this Wood? What a fool the human world made you. Your friendship is making your mind deteriorate. Do feelings so pollute you?" His words were delivered with surgical precision, eyes full of indifference.

My hand flies up to my mouth, and I gasp. Both? He plans to kill both of them.

"Why? You truly are a cold-hearted bastard." I spit out.

"That may be so, but I will also have the power to bring the humans to heel, finally. I will control them all, starting with Hawthorn. Imagine Fae being free to walk both worlds. No more hiding in the Wood. With all that power, I will be stronger than even Aurora and Poe," he says, drunk with his own machinations.

"Nix will never help you," I say vehemently.

"Oh, I think you'll find you are mistaken. Nix was so lost that it was easy to mold her into exactly what I needed her to be. Her newfound powers already darken her. Powers, I showed her how to use. Now she trusts me and only me after your stunt. It shouldn't be difficult to get what I want from her. I am in complete control with you out of the way—

no more of your foolish meddling. Nix will never suspect what I truly want from her. Zinn will be easily taken. She never received her full powers. Pity," he says and looks down to inspect his nails, "She is still stronger than most Fae, so once I drain them both, their combined power with mine will make me unstoppable," he says with finality, evil glinting in his soulless eyes, then sweeps out of the room as fast as he came.

Oh no. I am powerless to stop what is coming. No way out of this prison. I will lose them, both of them. I never even realized how sinister Briar truly was. I am such an idiot. Why would he hand the Wood over to someone with human blood? Anger and fear course through my body. How can I ever make things right? I may lose not only my friends, but the world will be as broken as my heart. I fall to my knees and scream into the darkness.

"Screaming won't help the situation," a voice comes from the corner of the room.

I squint into the room, dimly lit by torchlight, and I see him. Cadmun. Bound to the wall with unbreakable, enchanted manacles.

"Cadmun, oh no, I am so sorry. I thought the tear would work," I say and break down again, seeing his bruised and swollen face.

"No, it is my own fault. I thought it worked and let it slip what we did," he says, head bowed.

"Let's not play the blame game. That won't get us anywhere. We both took part," I say softly.

"What are we going to do, Ana?" Cadmun asks, sounding hopeless.

"What can we do? We are both stuck in here," I say, frustrated.

"I have to warn Nix," he says, then struggles with his chains, trying to break them, but no matter what he tries, they stay tight around his wrists.

"That is not helping. You are just going to hurt yourself, and I don't know if Nix can be saved," I say, and he stops struggling.

"What do you mean? Of course, she can. I saw her. I saw the real her. The tear worked. I had her back, but then she was gone again when she came back to her chambers with Lord Briar, who beat me as punishment." He says, full of anger.

The door bangs open, and Nix strolls in and stands in front of Cadmun, keys in her hand.

"I think you have learned your lesson. Now you can choose. Stay here with Ana and rot, or come with me and don't step out of line again," Nix says, voice sweet but devoid of kindness.

"Nix, listen, please. Lord Briar plans to kill you," I yell out to her.

"Don't talk to me. You don't get to talk to me ever again, traitor," Nix says and cuts her head towards me.

"No, Nix, please listen. He wants to kill you," I plead.

"Of course, you would say something like that. Your lies will not save you. You said you would never betray me again. You promised me, but look where we are now. If you want someone to blame, blame yourself," she says, her eyes cold but also hurt lurk in their depths. "Come, Cadmun. I forgive you, but as I said, do not try to change me again."

"Yes, Little Flower," Cadmun says and gives me a slight nod that I don't understand.

"Then come," she says, unlocking his restraints, "Follow me and don't speak," Nix commands.

Cadmun looks at me one last time, with determination in his eyes.

"Don't look at her. She doesn't exist," Nix commands, and his head turns forward, then he follows Nix out the door.

DANIEL

Zinn and a large man with pointed ears are pulling me along the streets. I am dazed and don't know what is going on inside of me. I feel full of fire, like I'm going to explode. The ringing in my ears is now a slight hum.

"How will we find him?" Zinn asks the man, urgency in her tone.

"He has probably gone into hiding," the man says.

"Then how is this going to work? We need him," Zinn says urgently.

"We will find him," the man says in a soothing tone.

We enter the playground behind the elementary school, and unease creeps into me. We bypass the swings and head into the forest behind the playground.

"Where are you taking me?" I ask, trying to get a hold of myself.

"We are taking you to someone who can help," Zinn replies, and we reach a circle made of clover.

I shrug them both off of me, then the ringing in my ears starts to return, and I ask,

"Who are you taking me to?" I realized this could be a mistake. "Not Doctor Fraund. I won't go back, I'm not crazy!" I shout.

"Daniel, look at me," Zinn says, then continues, "Please, there are things that won't make sense, but you need to understand we aren't going to hurt you. No, you are not crazy. You have magic flowing inside you, and we need to get it out of you. Do you feel like there is something moving under your skin? Do you feel off?" Zinn asks, concern lighting her grey eyes.

"Yes. How do you know that?" I ask, my fear telling me to stay and run at the same time.

Zinn extends her hand and points at the ground, and small white flowers appear right below her hand. I step back, shaking my head in disbelief. She reaches out to me and says,

"I know what it feels like because I have magic in me too. Please just come with us, we know someone who can help," she says, and I look into her eyes, and all fear, questions, and doubt want to disappear from my mind. I know I can trust her. I feel it. But I resist. I back up a step, look around, and ask,

"Why are we here? Where are you taking me?"

"Look, we don't have time. We need you to come. The magic might be killing you. Your nose is still bleeding. Daniel, please," Zinn pleads.

I reach up and wipe my nose. It comes away wet. I see the blood and vines start crawling up my legs. Fear seeps into me, and my ears begin ringing loudly. I fall forward and retch.

"Stop, Zinn, why are you doing that?" I yell.

"It isn't me! It's you, Daniel. You can't control the magic. We must get you to our friend Sky. He will know what to do," she says with urgency.

I finally take her hand. The large man is watching on with a pained look in his eyes. He shakes his head once and says,

"Come, we must go."

He grabs Zinn's other hand, and we step into the circle of clover as we reach the center. The world tilts. I feel faint and land on the ground so hard I bite my tongue.

"Brone! Watch out," Zinn yells at the man we are with.

Brone turns, then ducks, and a knife sails through the air and embeds itself in the tree directly behind me. Zinn runs towards the man who threw the knife and jumps in front of him. She roundhouse kicks him in the face, and he goes down hard. Zinn plants her foot in the man's chest, presses down, and I hear bones crack. Then she growls,

"Who sent you?"

Instead of answering, he grabs her foot and throws her back. Zinn lands hard on her back but recovers quickly. Then she pulls a knife from under her hoodie and launches it with deadly accuracy. The knife embeds in the attacker's chest, and he falls dead.

What the fuck did I just see? Fear spikes in my chest, and I scramble back until my back bangs into the tree with the knife still lodged in it.

"More Seekers approach," Brone says with urgency.

"How many?" Zinn questions, and she is shedding off her sweatpants and hoodie, revealing a tight leather outfit with knives strapped all over her torso and thighs. She retrieves the knife from the dead man. Lifts her hand, and the ground swallows him whole.

"Too many if we want to get the boy out alive," Brone says quickly, shedding his own clothing, also wearing similar leather clothing.

"To the trees?" Zinn says, making her way to me, placing her knife back into its sheath.

"No, the boy can't keep up, and the Seekers already tracked us there once," he says, quickly.

"So, what now?" Zinn asks, kneeling next to me.

"The Dark Tunnels," Brone says, and I don't like his tone.

"Daniel, are you ok?" Zinn asks, I am too stunned to speak, so I nod that I am ok.

"Come," Brone says and holds his hand to the ground. It groans, and I feel the air shift as I am met with a damp, musty smell, and he jumps in the hole.

"Here, you may need this," Zinn says, pulls the knife from the tree behind me, and holds it out to me.

I take it with my shaking hands.

"Why would I need this?" I ask, reeling from everything that just happened.

"You may need to protect yourself. Things aren't safe here. Hurry, we must go," Zinn says and pulls me to my feet.

"Hurry," Brone says from the darkness of the hole.

Zinn drags me behind her, and I slightly resist.

"Come on, Daniel, more of them will be coming," she says, frustrated, pulling on me harder.

"More what?" I ask relenting and follow her.

"Seekers. They are hunting us. We don't have time for this. Come on, jump," she says and leaps into the hole.

I look around and realize I am no longer at home, and I have no choice but to follow.

NIX

I walk the corridors of the palace, and Cadmun dutifully follows. It is a shame his face is marred by the punishment Lord Briar gave him. I don't even have to glamour him anymore. It is freeing not to have Ana's constant shadow lurking behind me, judging. She was never even that much help getting the other Fae to like me, as she had promised. I don't even care if they do now. I am so powerful that they dare not cross me. I like the way they part as I enter the ballroom, fear in their eyes. Some even bow their heads as I pass. My old self would have tried to disappear, blending into the walls. Now I hold my head high and will make them all bow one day. I walk to my throne and take a seat.

"Cadmun, sit," I say, and he does on the lush pillow I had placed at my feet for him.

"Dearest One, I am so glad to see your pet so well behaved," Lord Briar compliments me, but looks down at Cadmun in disgust.

"Yes, it is quite nice to have someone actually loyal to me by my side," I say, looking into Cadmun's eyes, and he stares back with what looks like longing.

"I need you to do something for me," Lord Briar says and turns to look at me.

"What would that be, my Lord?" I ask curiously.

"Come, let us talk somewhere with fewer ears," Lord Briar says, rising, and the whole court pauses to bow.

Jealousy runs through me, but I remember one day it will be my turn. I follow him out of the ballroom to his library, Cadmun staying close behind me. Lord Briar pauses at the door, and Cadmun and I enter, then he closes it. He crosses the room and takes a seat at his desk, then says,

"Have a seat, Dearest One."

Then gestures to the chair that is across the desk from him. I take a seat, then Cadmun comes to my side and takes a seat on the floor next to me.

"I need you to look for your sister," he says, leveling with a hard stare.

"Yes, of course. Where would you like me to go?" I ask, wanting to find Zinn, too. I need her power.

"Well, I don't need to go anywhere. I need you to enter the mind realm and bring her to us. Brone hasn't turned up with her yet. There is no other way to reach her physically at present. I need her to get you your full power. The time is coming for you to ascend," he says, and takes a key from his deep sleeve and opens a small chest that is next to Cadmun's book and the useless mirror from the human realm. He opens the lid to the chest, and I can't see what he is doing. I hear glass tinkling together, then he extracts a beautifully crafted blue crystal vial.

"This will take you where you need to go," he says and places the vial between us on the desk.

Cadmun tenses at my side at the sight of it.

"What is it?" I ask, scooting to the edge of my chair.

"This is Dream of Advaita. It aids in connecting minds. Your earlier attempts through your twin connection have not worked. This will give you the power to find her. You must take three drops: one to leave your mind, two to meet your target, and the third to return. Lie down. We only have five drops left, so you must succeed," Lord Briar says and leads me to a chaise lounge in the corner of the library.

I follow, and Cadmun stays close, a little too close.

"Cadmun, wait by the desk," I command, and he stops beside the desk, fear visible in his eyes.

I lie down, and Lord Briar hands me the vial. I tip it back, let three drops fall onto my tongue, and swallow. I hand it back to him, and he places it on the desk. My eyes flutter shut, and I feel a heavy weight run through my limbs. Fear spikes in me as I find myself falling into the dark, alone. My descent seems never-ending. I suddenly slow, and my feet touch something solid, and I look around. I recognize the space as the same dark place I was in before, when Zinn made her connection. Relief fills me. I know I am where I need to be. I call out into the black,

"Zinn."

Nothing, no response. I step further into the dark and search for her. Then I hear heavy breathing. I run toward the sound, and I see Zinn running in front of me. She suddenly stops and turns, looking confused.

"Zinn, it is time to face me. Why do you hide like a coward? You fear me that much?" I ask in a sharp tone.

"Nix?" Zinn asks, then she looks over my shoulder with fear in her eyes, she points behind me, and yells, "Run!"

I am thrust back into my body and bolt up. She pushed me out? It was as easy for her as flicking an ant off her arm.

CADMUN

Nix's eyes flutter shut, and fear and anger mix inside of me. I want to rush to her, but I am rooted in my spot by her glamour. He didn't warn her. The bastard. She could be stuck in her mind, forever lost. Minutes tick by. She looks like she is in distress, her face pinched at her brow. Lord Briar stands lurking over Nix, a wicked smile on his lips, enjoying the show. Just as I am about to give up, she sits up suddenly, gasping, eyes wild.

"What? What did you see?" Lord Briar demands.

"Zinn, I saw her, but she pushed me from her mind," Nix says in a rush.

I take my chance and quickly snatch the blue vial, stashing it in my pocket. I turn back to see Lord Briar's face twist in anger, I have seen before, and I brace for him to strike her, but the hit never comes.

"You failed," is all he says, slamming the chest shut and locking it and sweeping from the room.

I look to Nix and see rage burning in her eyes.

ZINN

I drop down into the tunnel and squint in the darkness, then Daniel jumps in and almost lands on top of me.

"Oof," Daniel grunts as he falls.

"I got you," I say and help him to his feet.

Brone is pulling dry tree roots from the ceiling and hands one to me. He cups his hands around the end, and a small flame catches it on fire. He quickly hands one to Daniel, and Brone does the same to Daniel's root, lighting its end with fire. While Brone busies himself with his own torch, I hold up mine and look at our path ahead, and I am rewarded with the sight of a maze of tunnels that lie before us. Brone holds his hand up and efficiently closes the hole we used to enter and says,

"Come now," in an urgent tone, I hurry after him.

"Why didn't we use the tunnels to get back to the human world?" I ask, irritated.

"No one uses these tunnels unless they have to," Brone says, sobering me.

"What do you mean?" I ask, feeling the air change, chilling me to the bone.

"Wait up," Daniel says, and I turn to see he has fallen behind and looks absolutely terrified.

I pause and wait for Daniel. Brone turns and says,

"We must keep moving. Dark creatures lurk in the dark."

"What do you mean, creatures?" Daniel asks, quickening his steps.

"Creatures of smoke and darkness that take the shape of dire wolves," Brone says, never slowing.

"Why did we come here then?" I ask, confused.

"Where would you have us go? We were about to be surrounded, and what would happen if the boy were taken to Briar?" Brone asks me pointedly.

"What about the path? The one Sky uses to lure in the Bleaker kids?" I ask, feeling the temperature drop even more.

"The Seekers will be watching that way as well. It is daytime, and humans usually go up when the sun is up, thinking it is safer. After helping us escape, Sky will be in hiding for a while," Brone says in a knowing voice.

"Do you know where he is?" I ask, trying to keep up, and I hear a distant howl.

Brone freezes and says,

"They caught our scent, Spirits be damned." Brone stops, turns to Daniel and me, and says, "We must move as fast as we can. You must not use magic. It draws them in."

"But if they sense magic, you are the only one who used any since we arrived," I cut at him.

"I used elemental magic to light the torches and seal the tunnel. That was small. They wouldn't have picked up our scent from that. What they really seek is Spirit magic, and your friend is almost leaking it out of his body, and they can smell it."

"It's my fault they can smell us?" Daniel asks with guilt in his eyes.

"I am sorry, but yes. Can you fight?" Brone asks with urgency still in his voice.

"Not really, I mean, I can take a tackle, but fighting no," Daniel replies, looking between us.

"He can throw knives with deadly accuracy," I tell Brone, remembering how Daniel can play darts.

"What, no, I can't," Daniel says, shocked.

"Yes, you can, you can throw a dart, you can throw a knife," I look to Brone, and he nods.

"Ok, I will go in point. You take the rear Zinn, and you, Daniel, keep up," Brone says, and we make our way forward on silent feet.

More howls sound from ahead, and Brone cuts right hard, and I bump into Daniel, and he drops his knife. I stop and help him pick it up, and I hear an eerie growling coming from a small opening in the tunnel wall to my left. I see yellow, animalistic eyes glowing towards me from the tunnel opening.

"What the fuck is that?" Daniel says, backing away.

The creature stalks forward, and I swing my torch towards it and yell,

"Run!" Over my shoulder to Daniel as I turn to face the creature.

I hear Daniel's feet moving further away, and then he yells,

"Brone!"

I plant my feet and am ready to fight the creature before me. It growls, drool dripping from its jaw, smoke and darkness rolling off its wolf-like body. I don't hesitate. I throw the torch at it, freeing both of my hands. The creature backs up, and I miss my target. The torch only grazes the wolf's shoulder. I pull both knives from my thigh sheaths and get ready to throw. The wolf lunges at me, and I quickly pivot, barely getting out of the way. The wolf turns to me, and I launch both knives. One embeds in the wolf's shoulder, and the creature turns quickly, and the second embeds itself into the tunnel wall. Ok, I can hit it. It isn't just smoke. I pull out two more knives. The wolf and I face off, circling one another.

"Zinn," Daniel shouts, and it rings through the air.

I turn and find Daniel and Brone rushing toward me with two creatures close behind them. Shit.

"Focus!" Brone shouts and turns to fight the two creatures coming his way.

My second focus is lost, and it costs me. The beast pounces, and I am pinned to the ground. I kick it hard in the stomach. It yelps, leaping off of me. Gouging open my thigh as it drags itself off of me.

BRONE

I see Zinn fighting one of the beasts, as Daniel and I race back toward her. Two of the foul creatures are closing on us. Zinn looks our way, and I yell for her to focus and turn to face my own foes.

I pull two daggers from my leather and throw one directly at the beast on the right. I make a clean hit to its neck, and it falls to the ground, limp. One down. The second wolf leaps at me, and I jump back, barely avoiding being clawed across the chest. I lash out with my blade and tear into the flesh of the beast's side. It yelps and dances to the side, oozing darkness from the wound.

"No! Zinn!" Daniel shouts. I turn to see her being tackled by the wolf she is battling. Fear tears into me. Zinn kicks the beast hard in the stomach, and it retreats. I turn back to my own beast. It is limping but still growling at me, ready to kill.

DANIEL

Zinn and Brone are fighting on either side of me. I don't know how to help. The creatures are terrifying monstrosities. How did I end up here? I will not die without fighting. I watch Zinn duck and dodge the beast she is fighting, blood dripping down her leg. Even though she is injured, she looks like a predator. Her confident and precise movements have me mesmerized. She lands a blow with her knife to the beast's side, then dances on quick feet back out of its striking range.

Looking at Brone, I see he has no problem keeping up with the beast he fights. He strikes a decisive blow with his fist to the snarling beast's face, and it goes down from the force, and Brone drives his dagger into its skull.

Turning my attention back to Zinn, she sidesteps the beast she is fighting, and it crashes into the wall where she had just been standing. It is stunned and stumbling to stand again. Zinn runs towards her, raises her knife to throw it. Suddenly, her eyes go glassy, and she falls. I see it happening. The beast takes its opening. Before I can think, I raise the torch in my hand, and I yell out, catching the beast's attention. It looks. I take the knife I have, holding the tip with my fingers, and launch it with everything in me toward it. The knife slams into the beast's skull and embeds itself to the hilt.

Ringing blasts into my ears. I fall to my knees. Holding my head, I look and see Zinn rising from the ground, yelling something I can't hear.

Then I hear it. A wolf's howl rings out loud and strong. Then a loud chorus of countless howls follows. The ground begins to rumble under my knees. Zinn points to something behind me. She stands and starts running at me full speed.

ZINN

Time stops, all goes black, and I fall into darkness, landing hard on the bottoms of my feet. Then I see Nix, standing before me. She steps toward me and says,

"Zinn, it is time to face me. Why do you hide like a coward? You fear me that much?"

"Nix?" I question. My eyes look past her in the dark, and I see them. So many of the wolves are running towards us. I point behind Nix and yell,

"Run!"

My eyes come into focus. I see Daniel on his knees, clutching his ears, and a large beast careens past Brone, heading straight for Daniel, howling as it approaches. Shit. I am not going to make it up in time. I stand as fast as I can, but I will be too slow. I take out one of my remaining knives and get ready to throw, but Brone is there first.

Brone tackles the huge wolf, and it flips over, pinning him beneath its front legs. No, this can't be happening. Howls are ringing all around us, and the ground is trembling. I raise my arm and throw with all my might, pushing with Wind, no point in holding it back now. The wolf's muzzle bends down and clamps onto Brone's arm. My knife embeds into the beast's eye socket, and it falls. Brone pushes it off, stands, holds his arm, and rushes to us.

Soil begins to cascade down upon us. Light seeps through the cracking ceiling. The ceiling begins to wrench open quickly, and then I see him. Sky. He lowers himself into the hole with a vine, takes in the situation, then pulls Brone, Daniel, and me towards him with vines. Then he pushes himself out of the hole. Sky uses his hold of the vines, and we are all pulled out of the hole behind him. He releases us with a quick wrist flick, then focuses on the hole and seals it tightly shut.

"I heard the beasts. What have you done?" Sky questions, then takes a quick look at us all, and his gaze lands heavily on Daniel, "He has broken the balance. Come, we must go."

BRONE

Sky pulls out of the hell we just experienced, and my arm screams in pain. I land hard on the ground. Sky takes one look at us all, his gaze landing on Daniel with an expression of knowing, and he says,

"I heard the beasts. What have you done? He has broken the balance. Come, we must go."

I rise as quickly as I can. Zinn pulls Daniel up, then looks to me and gasps and says,

"Your arm!"

Zinn rushes to me, and Sky moves to help Daniel stay standing.

"Here, we need to stop the bleeding," Zinn undoes one of the harnesses on her leathers, then quickly takes the strap and wraps it around my bicep and tightens it painfully. The blood flow stops immediately.

"Come, we really can't linger here. The Seekers have been searching for you," Sky says, then picks up a now unconscious Daniel, and throws him over his shoulder. Then he takes off on a strong gust of Wind. Zinn casts me a worried glance, and we both follow, pushing hard with the wind to keep up.

Paths appear for Sky in a way I have never seen before. The Wood is responding to him in a way I have never seen before. We travel in silence and reach a waterfall I have never seen before. Sky gently places Daniel on the ground. He begins making a complicated series of hand motions—the water parts, revealing a cave. Sky picks Daniel back up and gestures for Zinn and me to follow. We move to the cave, and the open curtain of water closes quickly. Sky expertly makes his way through the tunnels, and I see light ahead of us. We step out of the cave. I gasp at what I see.

A village stands before us with more humans than I have ever seen in one place before, milling about.

"Welcome to Solace," Sky says as he walks briskly towards a small cottage. An uneasy feeling washes through me as the humans stop to stare at our sudden arrival, alarm in their eyes. He steps inside the cottage. Zinn and I share a look before we follow.

ZINN

We follow Sky into the cottage. He places Daniel on the bed in the corner of the room. He turns to Brone and me and asks,

"Why were you in the tunnels?"

"We had to move fast, and we had no other choice. Seekers were going to surround us," Brone replies sharply.

"I still don't understand what those things are," I say, still shaken up.

"Those are the consequences of humans using magic. They were created by the corruption in human hearts, draining the Spirit from each other. Also, humans are drawing magic from the land, ultimately draining the very Spirit of the Wood. It is all a byproduct of Thorne's curse," Sky continues, and I notice Brone cradling his arm.

"Do you have anything I can use to clean up Brone's wound?" I ask urgently. Sky rushes to a cabinet in the kitchen, and I hear the noise of vials clinking.

"You don't have to do it. I can," Brone replies, looking at me with a look I don't understand.

"No, let me do this for you," I insist, inspecting the injury.

Sky returns with a vial of cleaning elixir, clean cloths, and a needle and thread. I busy myself cleaning Brone's wound. He hisses as I clean the wound with the elixir and begin stitching it up carefully. Once I am done, I clean my own wound to find it almost completely healed already.

"I still don't understand why they attacked us. We didn't use Spirit magic?" I question, cleaning the dried blood from my leg. Then I wash my hands in the cleaning solution and turn back to Brone.

"No, they were drawn to the boy. How did this happen? How does he hold such magic?" Sky questions, nodding toward Daniel, who is starting to stir.

"I think he absorbed it from the mirror Fiona created. He broke it by accident. Could that be it?" I ask as I finish dressing Brone's wound with a clean cloth.

"I see. Fiona did drain magic from you and place it in the mirror, giving it the ability to connect you to your sister through the veil of your two worlds," Sky explains.

I stand and move toward the bed, looking down at Daniel, and realize my carelessness caused this situation. If I hadn't left the mirror in his car, this would never have happened. Now his life is on the line, and I don't know if I can save him. Daniel slowly opens his eyes and looks around with wild eyes. He sits up quickly and then falls back onto the bed.

"Zinn! Are you ok?" He says in an anxious voice and looks me up and down, searching for any injuries.

"I am fine, calm down. We are safe now," I reply, squatting next to the bed and laying a reassuring hand on his shoulder. "How do we fix this?" I ask Sky desperately.

"He must give it to you. This is very important. If you forcibly take it, you may end up corrupting yourself and hardening your heart as hard as stone. You will lose yourself to darkness, Zinn. You have seen your sister, have you not? You must not try to pull it from the boy, or you risk draining his Spirit, not just the magic he has absorbed," Sky says with a weight to his voice, making me shiver.

"Can't you do it?" I ask, not wanting to risk hurting Daniel.

"No. It is not my magic to take. It comes from you and must be returned to only you. If someone else takes it, they risk the same fate, doomed to being corrupted forever."

"What if he keeps it?" I ask, trying to avoid causing any more damage to Daniel.

"I don't want it. Please take it. I think it is going to kill me. It hurts so bad," Daniel says, and moans.

"Ok. What do I have to do?" I ask, seeing that Daniel may be right. Noticing that his nose is crusted with blood, my fear spikes for him.

"Does the boy know how to use his magic?" Sky asks, face full of worry.

"No," is all I can say, hoping we can make this work.

DANIEL

Zinn says,

"No."

The truth of my situation is setting in. If I can't figure out how to give this magic back to her, I may die. The old Fae didn't deny it. It can't be taken from me. I don't know how this is going to work. I have no control over the magic as it is. The old Fae, they call Sky, approaches me and says,

"We must begin. We can't afford to wait any longer."

I sit up and nod.

"Just tell me what to do," I say, anxiety creeping into me.

"Zinn, come sit next to the boy," Sky says, and she moves and takes a seat next to me.

"Now what do we do?" I ask him.

"You must take each other's hands. Then, you, young sir, must try to transfer out your magic. You will feel it. Close your eyes and focus on the energy flowing through you. You will feel a separation between your own Spirit and that of the magic inside of you," he says, as if I should understand what he means.

"I don't understand what you mean. I will feel it?" I ask, getting frustrated.

"Takc a deep breath and clear your mind. You must look deep inside yourself. Close your eyes, reach out with your mind, and seek out what is not part of who you are. It will feel wrong and almost unwelcome, like it burns to brush your mind against it," Sky says, and I close my eyes.

I take a deep breath and try to do as he says and clear my mind, but fear and anxiety are a jumble in my head that I can't seem to get past. I open my eyes and tell him in a frustrated tone,

"I can't see anything. I am full of emotions I can't get past."

"Wait a moment, I may have what you need," Sky replies and goes to the cabinet in the kitchen, mumbling to himself.

"I am sorry, Zinn, I am trying," I say to her and look down, feeling defeated.

"No, I am sorry, Daniel. I never meant to drag you into any of this," she replies and softly touches my chin, tilting my head up to look at her.

Her smoky gray eyes look sad, and I want to do everything I can to take that pain away.

"Here it is!" The old Fae says triumphantly and quickly walks back to us.

Sky hands me a tiny green bottle and looks at me expectantly.

"Well, drink it," he says, frustrated.

"What is it?" I take the cork out and smell it. It smells strongly of fermented herbs.

"It is a calming draft. It will help your mind relax and open up your senses. There is no magic in it," he tells me, and I tip the liquid into my mouth.

I almost spit it out. It tastes so terrible, but I choke it down. Almost instantly, tension loosens from my shoulders, and I feel a weight I have been carrying for weeks lift off my chest.

"Ok, now try again. Close your eyes and look deep within," Sky instructs.

I do as he says. I take a deep, calming breath, and it is so much easier this time. My emotions are quiet. I search my mind and find myself thinking of Zinn. Zinn's beautiful eyes and her soft hands in mine, and I feel it. Something is pushing hard against my mind. The painful, burning sensation Sky spoke of is prodding at my brain.

"I feel it," I say, the pain increasing as I focus on it.

"Now you must push that out of you. Focus on pushing it to your hands and giving it to Zinn." Sky says gently.

I squeeze Zinn's hands tighter and begin to push. I meet resistance, and it won't budge.

"It won't let me push it out," I tell Sky, getting nervous again.

Now that I am aware of the sensation, I want it to be gone.

"Zinn, close your eyes and open yourself up. Let the energy flow into you, don't block it out," Sky says, then continues, "But under no circumstances pull it into you. You risk taking the boy's Spirit if you do."

"I understand," Zinn says, and her hands begin shaking in mine.

I push again harder this time. Still nothing. The power seems to be pushing back against my attempts to free myself of it. I dig deep inside me and push as hard as I can, gripping onto Zinn's hands. The power recedes slightly. I am panting with effort. I picture my hands placed against the burning sensation and shove one last time. Something clicks, and I feel power rush from me like a dam being broken open. Zinn gasps, and I hold her hands even tighter.

CADMUN

I stare down at my feet as I walk behind Nix to the bathing chamber. Nix has been sullen ever since her failed attempt to reach Zinn in the mind realm. Lord Briar has been keeping his distance as well. Which is a good thing for what I have planned. I clear my throat to get Nix's attention. She turns and waves her hand and says,

"You may speak."

"Would it be ok if I return to your chambers? I wish to avoid the other Fae," I lie.

"Why worry yourself with them? They don't matter. Now, no more complaining. Be silent," she commands.

Damn it. I just need a moment alone. I have to try to reach Zinn and warn her. If I can get to Zinn, maybe this can save Nix. Maybe Zinn doesn't care about breaking their connection anymore. There have been no sudden changes in their places since the night I was captured. Maybe the connection has already been broken. But Zinn did want to help Nix before. Maybe she will help me save her from Lord Briar. I won't know unless I try.

Fear claws down my back. I am running out of time. We enter the bathing chamber, and a few Fae bow their heads as Nix enters, and others glare. Nix removes her robe and steps into the tub.

"Cadmun, you may turn around. I know this makes you uncomfortable," Nix says, and I take one long look at her beautiful face before I turn my back on her.

I fiddle with the blue crystal vial in my pocket, knowing it is now or never. I pull the vial slowly out of my pocket and pause. I look one last time at Nix as she slides underwater slowly, then swims away. This is the last time I will see her, and I don't even get to say goodbye. This has to work. I must save her.

I put the vial to my lips. I take a deep breath, thinking of the girl I love. Then drink. One drop to leave. Two drops to meet. The vial falls from my hand, and the world goes dark.

ZINN

"It won't let me push it out," Daniel says, anxiety in his voice.

"Zinn, close your eyes and open yourself up. Let the energy flow into you, don't block it out," Sky says, then continues, "But under no circumstances pull it into you. You risk taking the boy's Spirit if you do."

"I understand," I say, and my hands tremble at the thought of pulling anything from Daniel.

Daniel's grip is getting painful as he tries to push the magic back into me. I feel nothing. Sky told me to open my senses. I am trying to do so while not focusing on the pain radiating from Daniel's grip on me. I breathe deeply and reach out my mind toward Daniel with everything I have. I am holding back my urge to pull anything from him in my desire to free him from the pain he is in. Pain that was ultimately caused by me.

A tingling sensation begins to prickle my skin. Then I feel something warm brush against my very soul. Something that feels familiar yet alien to me. Then all at once, I am hit with a wave of power that makes me gasp. My back arches. I can't do anything but surrender to the flow of power. The magic writhes beneath my skin, a living thing. I have never felt anything so beautiful but terrifying. The power soothes me, making me feel complete. Making me realize that this is what I have always been missing. I am coming together and coming undone all at once. The energy isn't slowing. It is an endless torrent, and I am beholden to it. I am screaming. My back arches even further from the strain, and everything goes black.

***

I am only breath. I am whole. I stand alone in the darkness, feeling no fear.

***

"Zinn," a voice calls.

Then I hear them. Voices. So many voices. I can't distinguish which one is calling me. I hear a scream. Then I hear Nix yelling,

"No!"

"Zinn!" I hear him, and I know who has come for me, Cadmun.

Cadmun's image comes into view. He is on his knees, holding his head in his hands.

"So many. I hear so many," Cadmun says, and looks up and spots me.

Shadowy figures surround us, and I hear discordant voices all around us. I walk to Cadmun and kneel beside him.

"Cadmun? Cadmun, what is happening?" I ask him urgently. His amethyst eyes are wild.

"Two. There were only two. Like you—two," he says, and he grabs his head again, "She needs you… Not safe… He is coming." Cadmun says and looks behind his shoulder. He turns back and says, "Only you can save her."

The voices begin retreating, the shadows vanishing, and someone is yelling my name.

BRONE

"Zinn!" I yell out before I can stop. Her back is bowed so far that I think it may snap. Then she goes slack. I run and catch her before she hits the ground, some of my stitches popping, but I don't care. She lands in my arms before making contact with the hard ground. She is breathing heavily, and her eyelids are twitching. I feel power buzzing below her skin, but she doesn't wake. Did it go wrong? I look and see that Daniel is also passed out on the bed.

"Give them a moment, Brone," Sky says, coming to place a hand on my shoulder.

I lift Zinn from the ground and place her in the chair standing beside the bed. I stand back, and anxiety pricks at my heart. I brush the hair out of her face and say,

"Zinn, come back." Her eyes fly open, a wild look in them.

"Cadmun no," she whispers. She looks into my eyes, and a single tear rolls down her cheek. "He is tired of waiting. We must save her," she says in her next breath.

"Who?" I ask, confused.

"Nix, we have to save her, Brone," Zinn says, and I know in my bones there is nothing I will be able to do to stop her.

NIX

Cadmun stares into my eyes as I walk into the tub with a strange look. The water feels so nice against my skin. I dive into the water and swim a bit farther into the large tub. The other Fae are staring at something beyond me as I come up, and I don't understand what they are looking at. Some are pointing past me, and I turn, and I see him. Cadmun. Cadmun is on the floor.

"No!" I shout.

I swim quickly back to the tub's steps and scramble out to his side. I run to him and kneel beside him, dripping water all over him and the floor.

"Who did this?" I growl out and level a stare at the other Fae in the room. They are all shaking their heads. "Tell me now, and I will let you keep your life."

"If it pleases my lady, your pet was standing there, and the next thing we knew, he just collapsed," one of the Fae replies, and the rest nod emphatically.

"Liars," I hiss.

I look down at Cadmun, and he is breathing steadily, but his eyes are twitching behind his eyelids as if trapped in a nightmare.

"Cadmun. Cadmun, wake up," I say, shaking him, and he doesn't respond.

No. No. No. I can't lose him. The kiss in my chambers, and 'Little Flower' whispered on his lips, all crash into my mind. I reach for his hand to take his pulse as I pick his wrist up, and a glinting object catches my eye. I see it, the crystal blue vial. My hands fly to my mouth. It hits me: three drops to return, and I scream, and it echoes off the walls.

DANIEL

I slowly open my eyes. I feel strange. The pressure in my head is gone. I sit up quickly and get lightheaded. I look around the room to find Zinn in a chair next to the bed, Brone and Sky standing in front of her, blocking my view. I am disoriented and notice things I didn't see before. There are no lights, just candles and a fireplace. Everything looks old, as if from another time. Then my focus returns to what just happened. The power is gone. My brain feels lighter, sharper. I want to ask if it worked, but I'm stopped by hearing Zinn say she needs to save Nix.

"Nix?" I question, and all eyes turn to me. "I thought you were her?" I say, feeling confused.

"Daniel, we need to talk," Zinn says, a hopeless look in her eyes.

"Come, Brone, we must talk," Sky says, and they duck out of the cottage, leaving Zinn and me alone.

"I don't understand. I thought it was just you. Who is Nix?" I ask, starting to feel like I may actually be crazy after all.

"I am going to explain things the best I can. You may not believe me, but I swear I am telling the truth," Zinn says in a serious tone, and I feel my heart rate pick up. "There is a Nix. She is my paternal twin sister."

Twin sister? What is she talking about? Then I remember the note from the mirror.

"The note. It said Nix had a sister. It was from a woman named Fiona claiming to be her mother. But isn't her mom's name Amanda?" I ask Zinn, feeling like I am about to hear something I may already know.

"No, Amanda is not Nix's mother. A woman named Fiona is. She is my mother, too. If you found a note in the mirror, it must have said something about me, Zinn," she explains.

"It said for Nix to wait for you and not go to the woods," I reply, remembering the note almost by heart. A chill runs down my spine, and the hairs on the back of my neck stand up.

"Well, you probably mean the Wood. The realm we are currently in is called the Wood. So let me ask you, did you ever look in the mirror?" Zinn asks me with a weighted look in her eyes.

"Yes," I reply, not wanting to remember the moment my world began to spiral out of control.

"What did you see? Did you see your reflection?" she asks me, and the memory of seeing her reflected back, singing, pops into my mind.

"No, I saw you. Why did I see you?" I ask more curiously than scared.

"Well, that mirror was full of magic. It was one of two mirrors, and the mirrors connected me to Nix and her to me. There was an accident when I was very young. I used the mirror when I wasn't supposed to, and it made it so Nix and I would trade places," Zinn says, looking full of guilt.

"What do you mean, trade places?" I ask, confused, feeling like I am losing it all over again.

"Well, we would switch our minds into each other's bodies. It is hard to explain," she says, frustrated.

"You mean like the movie 'Freaky Friday'?" I interrupt, trying to understand.

"Yes! Exactly like that. Just know there is a Nix, but the girl you spent time with was me. I was in Nix's body most of the time we were together, not Nix. The time she, well, I guess I should say I broke your arm, when you almost hit me with your car, being lab partners, and Hawkes, it was me, not her."

"So, was any of it real?" I ask, feeling anger rising in me.

"Yes, it was real. It was as real to me as it was to you," Zinn says, and a tear slides down her cheek.

"Don't do that," I say, in a sharp voice.

"Don't do what?" she asks, confused.

"Cry. You were lying to me the whole time! You were not even real. Nix was real. Now what am I supposed to do?

The whole town thinks I am crazy, and Nix doesn't even exist there anymore!" I say standing too fast in my anger, but falling back to the bed when a wave of dizziness hits me.

"What do you mean, the whole town?" Zinn asks freezing.

"No one, not the cops, not the doctor, or even Seth, remembers Nix. Nothing about our time together exists any more than Nix does," I say, my fear of going home and still being thought of as crazy is rising to the surface.

"They glamoured the whole town?" Zinn says to herself more than to me, and looks like she is going to be sick.

"What does that even mean?" I spit. Remembering all the reasons, I have to hate the girl sitting in front of me.

"They made everyone forget. That is something that Fae can do, a kind of magic," Zinn explains, standing and then starts to pace in the small space.

"So, you can fool people into believing what you want them to believe? Why would I remember then if no one else does? That makes no sense," I say, wanting to be anywhere but here, and start to move toward the door.

"It must have been the magic that was inside of you. It was my Fae magic," she says, and it seems like she isn't sure of the answer either.

"You know everyone in town thought I was crazy! I was locked up in that hospital for days, and no one believed me. Do you know what that feels like? To be that alone?" I shoot at her.

"Yes. I do know. Why do you think I was with you to begin with? You may not fully understand, but for the first time in a long time, being with you made me feel. Well, seen by someone," she says, and has hope in her voice.

"That seems pretty selfish if you ask me. You deceived me from the very beginning. None of this was ever real," I say, trying to make my words sting.

"No, please understand I never tried to lie to you. Yes, it was selfish," Zinn admits.

I pause and turn back, and see she is crying. Tears freely flow down her cheeks. My mind jumps, and I am back in the moment, standing in the street, looking down at her in my arms. Worried I had hurt her with my car. The way her hands felt on my face, and my anger receded slightly. I look into her eyes and say,

"All of this doesn't make sense. I don't even understand why any of this happened to me."

"I don't know what to say. I never meant to hurt you, Daniel. I never thought you would be dragged into this world," Zinn says, wiping her face with the back of her hand.

"So, what happens now? Am I stuck here? I can't unsee any of the things I have been through," I say, scared. I may have to spend the rest of my life in this upside-down world, or go home and carry all these secrets with me.

"No, you aren't stuck here," Zinn replies in a rush.

"Then I want to go home. But I don't know how I am supposed to forget the horror you have subjected me to," I tell her honestly.

"That's the thing you won't remember. We can make you forget," she says, sadness lacing her voice.

"I will forget it all? Even the good?" I ask because I realize some things I might not want to forget.

"Yes. Everything, even the good," Zinn says sadly.

Part of me is torn knowing I may lose the memories of the girl I loved. But I also realize that the girl was never real.

"Then do it. I don't want to stay here. I want to go home," I reply, wanting to put this behind me. My heart fractured by loss and anger.

ANA

I am slowly going crazy in this damn cage. I have tried to get out so many times that I think I have given myself electroshock therapy. I need to get to Nix. That bastard Briar is going to kill her. Not only has he stolen my friend, but he has also changed her completely.

Does she want to be saved? I don't care what she has become. I can't let her die. How do I get to her?

Then there is Zinn. Is Zinn actually the one I love? My mind swirls with memories of my years with Nix. How would I ever really know who I was with?

Frustrated, I kick my plate of mush they gave me for breakfast. It doesn't matter anymore who I love. This is bigger than my feelings. Things are so much worse than I thought they could ever be. Briar doesn't just want control of the Wood. He wants control over the world. I must get out of here. Fuck. What am I going to do?

May enters to collect my dish, as she does three times a day. She lingers by the cage door, noticing the mess I have made. May steps in and closes the door behind her. May doesn't fear me. I have never tried to attack the poor woman. The woman Nix drained as practice. How could I ever be cruel to her? She begins cleaning the mess, and something clicks in my mind. I may know how to get out of here after all.

BRONE

"What are we going to do?" I ask Sky, knowing Zinn well enough, to know her mind is set on saving Nix.

"Zinn has a choice she must make before we make any plans," Sky replies cryptically.

"What choice? It is clear she is going to try to save her sister," I cut at him, then the cottage door opens.

I watch as Zinn slowly walks out of Sky's cottage. Zinn has a look, I would know anywhere. Loss. I stop myself from going to her. Daniel follows on her heels, and I see confusion and rage on his face. I bristle slightly, but then I deflate. Zinn is not mine.

Zinn reaches us and says to Sky,

"I need your help. Daniel wishes to go home. He also wants his memory erased," she says, and I see she has been crying.

"I see. Is that your choice, truly?" Sky says, turning to Daniel.

"Yes," is Daniel's only reply.

ZINN

"Yes," Daniel says, and it hits me like a gut punch.

"We must not linger then," Sky says, and he walks toward the cottage.

We all follow Brone, trailing behind me. As Daniel enters the cottage, Brone places his hand on my shoulder. As soon as I register the feeling, he breaks contact, and I almost wonder if I imagined it. I step into the doorway of the small cottage and linger by the door uncomfortably as Sky rummages around, packing a small pack of supplies. Daniel keeps glancing my way, as if he is about to say something to me, but he never does.

"Ok, young sir, time to go," Sky says, and the finality of everything sets in.

"How will you get him home?" I ask Sky, worrying they may try the tunnels again.

"The Wood has many secret paths only I know. I shall get him to the portal safely. You have my word, Zinn," Sky says, and I believe every word.

"And I won't remember anything?" Daniel asks quietly.

"No, you will not. I will pluck all the twins' memories from your mind. Then stay only long enough to clean up any loose strings that remain in your world," Sky says to Daniel, reassurance in his voice. "Brone, Zinn, you must make haste. Time is running short for Nix. I feel the Wood shifting. You will find everything you need for your journey in my cottage. Here, take this," Sky says and hands me a small piece of rolled parchment.

"What is it?" I ask about unrolling it.

"It is a map. Follow the routes I have marked, and your trip to the Great Tree will be as smooth as possible. We must go now, young sir. Zinn, you have two choices before you. If you remember, to keep the balance, you may do more than you think possible for us all," Sky says and gives me a wink.

"What does that mean?" I say, but Sky doesn't stop to answer.

I turn to look at Daniel, following behind Sky, and Daniel's back to me. It is the last thing I see of him, before he disappears into the tunnel toward his home. Daniel will go home and forget, and I will remain here and remember. Tears pool in my eyes. I turn so that, Brone can't see. He was never really mine to have. I belong here, and I know my path forward will never lead back to him.

NIX

I cradle Cadmun's head in my lap. May approaches and places my robe around me, and I shoo her away.

"Wait, May, can you get someone to help me move him to my room?" I ask hastily.

"Yes, Mistress," she replies and turns and quickly hurries away.

Fae look, on with disgust in their eyes. One hurries away, looking back at the scene with a wicked glint in his eyes as he takes me in. I don't care what they think. Let them judge me. I place Cadmun's head gently on the ground and wrap my robe around me, feeling colder than I ever have before. I reach down and sweep Cadmun's hair from his forehead and feel if he has a fever. There isn't one. I have tried everything to wake him, and he stays still. Only his eyes are moving under his eyelids, trapped in another world.

May comes back with two men servants on her heels.

"Here they are, Mistress," May says, and backs out of the way.

"Take him to my chambers," I command, and the two men do as I ask and lift Cadmun from the ground.

I pick up the blue vial that is beside Cadmun and quickly place it in my pocket. The door to the bathing chamber flies open, and Lord Briar strides toward me quickly, a dark look in his eyes. The Fae that rushed from the room moments ago is following on Lord Briar's heels with a triumphant look in his eyes.

"What is the meaning of this?" Lord Briar demands, taking in the scene before him.

"Cadm… My pet is ill," I say, realizing my mistake.

I almost said Cadmun's name, so I quickly calmed my tone to indifference.

"I am just having him removed to my chambers," I say as an explanation for what he is seeing, and I sweep past him.

"Well, just drain him and be done with him. You can find a new pet," Lord Briar says, looking at Cadmun with disgust.

I turn quickly to tell him I will do no such thing. My robe flares around me, and the vial flies from my pocket. It lands on the ground and rolls to Lord Briar's feet. He bends down, picks up the vile, and levels me with a stare. I tense waiting for the hammer to fall.

"Hahaha, you think you can deceive me, Dearest One?" he laughs, and his pet name for me holds no humor, though.

"Deceive you how? My pet is ill. I will do what I wish with him, I am sure he will wake soon," I say, and realize how much I want that to be true.

"Dearest One, do you not see? There was no third drop. He will remain how he is until his body grows weak and he dies," Lord Briar smiles in a cruel way I have never noticed before. "Do what you wish with your pet," he all but spits the last word.

Then, a split second of what looks like worry flashes in his eyes as he looks at the vial in his hand. The look is gone before I am sure it was even there, and he pockets the bottle, then sweeps from the room as fast as he came.

ZINN

I can no longer look toward the tunnel where Daniel just disappeared through. He just disappeared from my life forever. I turn and stalk in from the doorway of the cottage, knowing Sky will have the supplies we need there. I need to find replacements for the weapons I lost in the tunnel. I turn and see Brone is tentatively looking at me.

"Well, are you coming in?" I ask him, and his eyebrows raise.

Brone strides toward me, and I pause to let him catch up. I hold out the map to him and say,

"Can you read this? I don't know my way around the Wood."

"Yes, I can do that," Brone replies and takes the map, his hand brushing mine.

I walk through the door and start immediately rifling through a large chest by the door. I don't find any weapons, but I find a new set of fighting leathers. These are white and older than any I have ever seen before bust still in great shape. I begin changing quickly out of my shredded pants, and Brone says,

"I have never seen this route before."

"But you can read it, right?" I ask, frustrated as I change into the matching top, buckling all the harnesses for weapons across my chest and thighs.

"Well, yes. I just don't know what dangers will lurk in these parts of the Wood," he says, and I turn to face him.

His eyes go wide at the sight of me, and I say,

"What?"

"You look like a true warrior of old in those leathers," he says, then quickly turns back to the map.

I am confused by what he means by 'of old', but I don't have time to ask. I turn and look around the room, see another chest by the foot of the bed, and head over, hoping to find weapons. I open it and find more clothing. I see another set of white leathers and realize they will fit Brone, and I toss them to him. They bounce off him and hit the floor. He is still transfixed by the map. Sky said everything would be here, damn it, but where? I circle the small room and notice an empty pack. I snatch it, say,

"Here, Brone, fill this with food, and anything you think will be useful for the journey."

I turn to toss it to him, and he is half-dressed, and I can't help but admire his bare torso. He looks at me I turn away quickly. I scan the room one last time and spot another trunk. I really hope it will have what we need. I rush over to it and throw open the lid. Jackpot. I pull out four throwing knives and place them in the sheaths on the top of my leathers. I dig carefully through the sharp weapons, then find two daggers and place them in my thigh sheaths. At the very bottom of the chest lies a large, broadsword with a silver hilt encrusted with gems. It seems to call to me. I now regret never learning how to work with that type of weapon, so I call Brone over and say,

"Do you know how to use this?"

He pauses, filling the pack with food and first-aid supplies, then walks over to see what I am talking about.

"I haven't seen a sword like that in a very long time. It is imbued with the power to help your aim be true. It reacts to the magic that a Fae naturally carries. The stronger the magic in the bearer, the more accurate it will make your aim."

"Can you use it?" I ask again, realizing why I felt a pull to the sword.

"Yes, I can wield such a weapon," he replies, and I hand it carefully over to him.

He deftly swings the sword side to side and feels its weight, then says,

"This truly is an amazing weapon."

I look one last time in the chest and spot the scabbard and strap that must belong to the sword, and hand it to Brone as well. He makes quick work of strapping the sword to his back. I turn and grab one more small knife and place it in my boot.

"You should look through here and get what you need," I say, and go check what he has packed for our journey.

I see he has thought of everything. I pace impatiently while he straps weapons to himself.

"How long will the journey take?" I ask, picking up the map from the table.

"Half a day at most. The map is actually leading us to a portal that will take us to the Great Tree, cutting our trip down by two days," he replies, and I see him clearly for the first time.

***

I see myself reflected in his garnet eyes and know he won't let me down.

BRONE

"We should move as quietly as possible on this journey. I am not sure what lurks on the path we are to follow," I tell Zinn.

"I agree. You take the lead," she replies, and she grabs the pack, and we head out.

Zinn and I head toward the tunnel, leaving Solace behind us. We reach the waterfall, and it parts for us. Once on the other side, I hold up my hand for Zinn to stop. I scan the area for any Seekers that may be around. I hear nothing, which I take as a good sign. I turn to Zinn and nod, letting her know it is all clear. She nods back, letting me know she understands. I look at the map, take the left path, then tuck it into my pocket.

The greenery retreats for us in the way it does for Sky. I am slightly nervous to have to follow an unknown path. Sky left without a word about what we might encounter on our journey, and it's putting me on edge. We follow the path for a few miles, and the greenery stops separating for us. I pause, pull out the map, and see we need to change directions. Zinn suddenly is at my side and whispers,

"Do you hear that?"

I freeze and listen, then I hear it. Hooves and a lot of them. We have entered the centaur's territory.

ANA

I pace in my cage waiting for May to make one of her three daily appearances. I am not considered important enough to have a guard outside my cage. I only see May. She is my only contact with the outside world. May enters with my fresh bowl of slop, which they have been feeding me.

"Hello, May," I say, and it startles her.

I haven't actually tried talking to her in a while. I used to beg her to get me out of this place, but she would remain silent and quickly enter and exit my cage to exchange my food bowls. As expected, she ignores me. I back up in the cage, letting her have room. As she opens the door, I let my hand casually graze the bars. I brace myself for the shock that usually comes. To my surprise, I feel nothing, and I smile. The door closes behind May, and I am instantly shocked by the bars. I yelp, startling her, and she jumps back toward the door and scurries out quickly, forgetting my old bowl in her hurry to get out of the cage.

I am forming a plan as she hurries out of the room where my cage is.

Don't worry, Nix, I still might be able to help you.

ZINN

"Centaurs," Brone says, in his gravelly voice.

"We need to hide. When Nix first came to the Wood, one attacked her," I say, quickly.

Brone aims his hand toward the ground, and I stop him. After being in the tunnels, the last place I want to go is underground. I place my hand on his shoulder, shake my head no, and point to the trees. He nods in reply. Then he scoops me up and launches us into the trees. We reach the dense canopy. He places me gently down on a branch thick enough for both of us to stand comfortably. I weave my hands around, guiding my power to create a dense vine enclosure around us.

Hooves beat closer, and a herd comes into view below us. There are at least ten of them. My heart is beating wildly in my chest. They gallop around the clearing and form two groups that face each other. A large male with blonde hair and a long beard steps forward in the circle and begins pawing at the ground, and says,

"You took your fill last time. It is our turn to get the spoils this time."

"That human barely had enough Spirit to go around. We will have the next one as well," a ginger-colored-haired female says, stepping forward.

"You want to go against the code? I will defend our claim when the time comes," the blonde says, circling the ginger-haired female centaur.

The female turns sharply and punches the blonde male in the sternum, and he grunts. She rears up onto her hind legs and stomps down hard on her front hooves, her eyes daring him to question her again. He sidesteps a few paces away from the female, then begins sniffing the air above him.

"You smell that? It is faint, but it is human," he says, and begins to approach the base of the tree we are in.

Me! They smell me. My half-human side must be detectable by them. Brone looks down, then looks at me, and I know he has just had the same realization. He moves faster than humanly possible and presses me against the trunk of the tree, covering my body with his large frame. My breathing is heavy. I am trying to calm myself, but it gets worse. Brone takes his hand and tilts my chin, so I am looking at him, and I see his calm, steady gaze. I take a deep breath and exhale, and his eyes dip to my lips, then his eyes dart quickly back to my eyes.

"Don't pretend like you smell a human! You know they never get this deep in the Wood. You are just too much of a coward to face me," the female spits and continues, "Let's away, there are nothing but fools here."

The female and the five Centaurs that were behind her take off deeper into the Wood toward the way we came.

"I swear there was a scent, but now it is gone," the male says and slams his fist into the tree, his knuckles coming away bloody.

"Come, we can't let them claim the next human," the blonde says, to his herd.

"Didn't Lord Briar promise that we would have plenty of humans in the coming days?" A black-haired female asks.

"Yes, but that is only if he has the two girls, not just the one," the blonde replies with frustration in his voice.

"Maybe we should just wait," the black-haired female offers.

"No, we will get what is ours. Let's go, they are getting too much of a head start," the blonde says, and they all gallop off in the same direction as the other herd.

Brone and I stay perfectly still, staring into each other's eyes for a few seconds, making sure the Centaurs will not return. Brone gives me a slight nod and backs up, freeing me from the cage of his body. I feel a chill from the lack of his body heat and shiver slightly.

"Did you hear what they said?" I ask Brone quietly.

"Yes, Briar needs you both. Are you sure you want to save Nix? This could be a trap," Brone says with concern in his voice,

"Cadmun wouldn't lead me into a trap. If it comes to it, I will fight Lord Briar myself. I will not let her be corrupted any longer. If Cadmun had hope, then I must have hope as well. I must be there for Nix, even if she hates me. I don't want her to die," I say, and I know it is the honest truth. Nix can't die. I wave my hand toward the vines and open our enclosure. We climb quickly from the tree and run in the direction marked on Sky's map, the greenery parting for us once more.

NIX

I watched as Cadmun's chest rose and fell all night. The steady rhythm calmed my fear that he might be lost for good. What have I done? How could I parade him around and treat him like a pet to be controlled? Better yet, why did he let me? The Cadmun I remember never backed down from a fight. Well, except for maybe with me. Not Zinn but me. He was always on my side, even when Zinn was in my body. He was the first to listen. I take his hand in mine and squeeze tight, hoping he can hear me, and I lean to his ear and whisper,

"Thank you, Cadmun. You are the only one who saw me. I am so sorry. Please come back."

He doesn't stir. He remains in his state of perpetual sleep. I lay my head on his chest, and for the first time in a long time, I start to cry.

The door bangs open, and Lord Briar enters. He takes in the scene before him, and looks down his nose at me and says,

"I thought I taught you better than this, Dearest One."

The pet name is making my skin crawl, with how wrong it feels, hitting my ears.

"Come, I need one last thing from you, then you can come here and rot with the boy for all I care," he says, and I get chills.

"What do you mean by the last thing?" I ask, dreading his answer.

"You will see, come now," he says with finality.

I wait until he exits the room, and I press a soft kiss on Cadmun's lips, realizing this may be the last time I see him. I stand and leave my chambers and the one I love behind.

ANA

I have been pacing for hours. I have the extra bowl May left in my cage, discreetly tucked under my arm. I wait for another eternity. The door finally opens, and May walks in. She has my fresh food. She takes another eternity to reach my cage, and she unlocks it, and I take my chance. I launch the empty bowl, and it lands perfectly. It is wedged between the cage side and door, keeping the electrical field down. I turn to May and say,

"Sorry about this," and knock her out cold.

I grab the key from her dress pocket and take her cloak. I throw it over my shoulders, clasp it around my neck, and hide my very noticeable hair under the hood. I stuff the key in my pocket, so May can't escape and alert anyone about my newfound freedom. I scramble to the cage door, wrenching it open, and the bowl clatters to the floor.

Once I am in the hallway, I try to blend into the walls as May does. I try to make myself as invisible to the other Fae as I possibly can. None of them seems to notice my presence. They all seem to be excited about something happening in the ballroom. They are all wearing matching black cloaks and are chattering excitedly. It gives me the creeps. I make a break for the hallway to Nix's room and find it blessedly empty. I push the door open, and I am so stunned I freeze in my tracks.

Cadmun… He is lying in the bed, pale as a ghost, not moving. I rush over, thinking the worst, but as I reach his side, I see he is still breathing. I sigh and look widely around the room for Nix, but she isn't here. Where could she be? Did she do this? Dread pure dread hits me. All the Fae dressed in black passed me, all going the same direction. I know exactly where to find her, and I hurry from the room. I hope I'm not too late.

BRONE

We don't have much further to go, and everything is quiet. This part of the Wood feels untouched—secret. I slow my pace as we reach the end of the map that Sky gave us, and I turn around, looking frustrated. We aren't at the portal.

"I think we are lost," I tell Zinn, as she steps beside me.

"What do you mean?" Zinn says, sounding anxious.

"Well, he said it would only take half a day. The day is almost over, and this is where the map leads," I say, frustrated that I got us into this mess.

"Wait, do you hear that?" Zinn questions, and the leaves near us begin to rustle.

"One is not lost when the path doesn't want to be found," a silky female voice purrs.

Then, a being I have never seen before steps from the shadows. It has the head of a beautiful woman, the body of a large lion, and beautiful wings tucked neatly to its sides.

"A Sphinx," Zinn whispers, and I don't recognize the word.

"Very good, young one. I have not seen any other Fae in many ages. Tell me what it is that you wish?" the Sphinx asks curiously.

"Don't tell it anything," I say and pull the sword from my back.

"I don't think Sky would have led us to a fight," Zinn says, and places a hand on my shoulder.

"You know the one who knows the paths? He is the one who sent you? Then it is the passage you seek," the Sphinx says, sitting on her haunches.

"See, Sky did mean for us to come here," Zinn says, and I relax slightly, putting my sword down.

"If it is the passage you seek, you must pass my test. Only a worthy mind can pass," the Sphinx says, with a knowing look.

"What test?" I ask, nerves prickling my spine.

"Answer my riddle, and you may pass through the portal," the Sphinx says, and steps aside, showing us a circle of dense clover.

I immediately recognize it is a portal.

"Let's just make a run for it," I whisper into Zinn's ear.

"To run would be death, my pretty face may fool you, but I will end you with my claws," the Sphinx says, hearing my whisper somehow.

"What is your riddle?" Zinn asks cautiously.

"Once asked, you must answer. I will wait as long as it takes for your answer, but answer wrong and your fate is death," the Sphinx warns.

"I am ready," Zinn says, before I can stop her.

I am filled with apprehension, but I must trust that Zinn is making the right choice.

"You have been warned of the consequences. Solve the riddle, and you may pass. Here is my question:

What carries weight in the present, but cannot be measured by any scale?

You may speak to each other to solve the riddle, but once you make your final answer, I will make my judgment." The Sphinx says, and my heart drops.

What does that even mean? I think long and hard, and I whisper to Zinn,

"Do you think it could be air?"

"Well, I am not sure that is quite right. In Nix's world, you can measure air," Zinn replies and looks to her feet, eyes focused on the question before us.

"Measure air, how is that possible?" I question her.

"One of you will choose correctly. You already have the answer tight in your mind," the Sphinx says, in a low tone.

"That doesn't matter right now, focus, Brone. We are running out of time to get to Nix, I can feel it," Zinn says in a slightly frustrated tone.

I am thinking long and hard, and one answer comes to mind, but I am scared to say the word out loud. I steel myself and whisper to Zinn,

"What about love?"

Her head swivels toward me, and a blush flushes her face.

"I think you are on the right track, but it doesn't feel right," she says, looking at her feet again.

I think about what the Sphinx said, and I realize that Zinn will know the answer.

"I think you know the answer," I say to her, and she looks up at me, worry etched on her face.

"What if I am wrong? We will die, and Nix will be lost," she says, with anxiety in her tone.

"I trust you," I say, with conviction in my voice.

"Ok, I am ready," Zinn says, and steps toward the Sphinx.

"Are you sure? There is only one answer I will accept," the Sphinx warns.

"I am ready," Zinn says, determination in her voice.

"Your answer?" the Sphinx asks.

"Memories," Zinn says, and a strong Wind swirls around us.

"You have chosen the right. You may pass," the Sphinx says, moving aside from the portal and allowing us to enter.

"Hurry, Brone, I have a bad feeling we may be too late. I feel a fear that is not mine," Zinn says, grabs my hand, and pulls me to the portal.

ZINN

We step into the portal. The world tilts, and we land in front of the Great Tree, and I feel a pull I can't explain. It is too cold outside, and I see my breath coming out like smoke.

"Something is not right. The air is strange," Brone says, striding toward the tree.

He lays a hand on the trunk, looks around, and is unnerved when a door appears before us.

"I do not know where Nix is," Brone admits.

"It is ok. I can feel her follow me," I say, and take the lead.

I run, pushing myself with Wind, and Brone follows quickly behind me. In this moment, I don't need a map or him to guide me. I can feel Nix's fear calling me. We round a corner, and I slam into someone.

ANA

I crash into someone hard, and I fall.

"Ana?" a voice says, and I know exactly who it is.

"Zinn, hurry, we need to get to Nix," I say, with urgency in my voice.

Zinn pulls me up and takes off in the direction of the ballroom, Brone following on her heels, with a large sword strapped to his back. Zinn is gone before I can warn her that Briar needs her to complete his plan.

Fear claws at my chest, and I run, struggling to catch up.

BRONE

We enter the antechamber, and I see four guards stationed in front of the doors. Zinn skids to a stop, then, without hesitation, she launches two daggers in quick succession at a guard approaching her. He falls. I run, pulling the sword from my back. I send my Spirit into it, and it hums like meeting an old friend.

I approach the guards and dispatch one coming at me with one swift blow. He falls instantly. The sword is guiding my aim with deadly accuracy. Zinn struggles with two guards blocking her way to the ballroom doors. She is fighting fiercely with her daggers in her hands. I come up behind the guard closest to me, and he senses my presence and spins. Our swords clash.

"Zinn, go! I will handle them," I yell, parrying the blows my attacker aims at me.

Ana finally catches up and screams,

"He wants you both," but Zinn has already blasted the doors open with such force with Wind that all of us in the antechamber fall.

Ana and I jump to our feet, the guards righting themselves and heading after Zinn.

"Give me a weapon," Ana yells, and I toss her a knife, and she catches it in midair.

Ana flips the knife in her hand, so she is holding the blade, and launches it toward the guard who has rushed after Zinn. The knife embeds in his back, and he goes down. I jump and flip in the air over the last guard, blocking him from catching up to Zinn. I thrust my sword into his chest he crumples to the floor. I look up and see Ana has already made it to the ballroom. I rush to catch up, not knowing what I am running into.

NIX

Dread fills me as I follow Lord Briar toward the ballroom. All the Fae we pass are clad in black robes and whispering to each other. What did he mean by 'one last thing'? Is he going to crown me today? But don't we need Zinn's power? We walk into the ballroom, and I see the throne I usually sit on has been moved to the center of the room. All the banquet tables are gone. The room is just full of a sea of Fae in black bowing at Lord Briar's entrance. The sight of them making the hairs on the back of my neck stand on end.

"Come, Dearest One, have a seat, won't you?" Lord Briar instructs more than he asks.

"What is this about?" I ask him, taking my seat as he instructed.

"The time has come for you to take your proper place among our people," he says, and walks to stand in front of his throne.

I don't feel any relief from my anxiety that is knotted in my stomach. Something is off in Lord Briar's eyes. He is looking at me, like I am the cake. More Fae trail into the room, and the doors are shut. Alarm bells are going off in me, and I know I am not about to receive the crown I was promised.

"Welcome all," Lord Briar's voice booms through the room. "Today, Nix will truly become one of us. Nix holds the key to what we have been searching for. She holds the power to free us forever from the human blight that we must endure," he continues, and some Fae in the crowd hiss at the word humans. "Nix, far too long have your kind kept us trapped in the Wood. Lucky for me, you are part of the key to our freedom. I had planned to wait until your sister was returned to us, but I find I grow bored of waiting. Once I have your power, I will easily overtake her. It is a shame she never came into her true powers, but I have made you strong enough to make up for what she lacks. I will end both of you. You are both an abomination to our kind and unworthy of the power you carry. So today, my loyal Fae watch as I bring about a new era for our kind," he finishes, and turns a hard gaze on me.

"What are you talking about? You were going to make me Lady of the Wood, you said I would take the throne," I say, in the strongest voice I can muster, but fear is clawing at the back of my neck.

"Oh, Dearest One, you will never wear a crown except the feeble one braided into your hair. Stay still, this may hurt," he says, extending his hand toward me, and I begin to feel a pull inside me.

"No!" I yell and stand bracing against his attempt to drain me and throw the vines that adorn my arms at him, but he swipes his hand, and they disintegrate into dust.

I pull water from the ground, form it into hundreds of sharp icicles, and launch them at him. He swipes his hand, and most burst into harmless snow, but one grazes his cheek, causing a small cut to appear. The crowd gasps, and he wipes his cheek. He examines the blood that drips from the cut as if it were the first time he has ever seen any of his own blood. His face goes from amused to rage in a matter of seconds.

"You will regret doing that," he says, his voice full of venom.

A large piece of marble from the floor rises in the shape of a hand and wraps around me. It begins to squeeze the breath from me. I try to react, but Lord Briar raises both his hands, and the feeling of hooks pierces through my very being. They claw in burrowing for the power inside me, causing me to scream. The pain is excruciating. I can't take it. I feel the drain begin and almost want to beg for mercy. I am trapped, and no one can save me. I think of him then, Cadmun—his warning. I am a fool. Now Cadmun is lost to the mind realm, and if it is my last moment in this world, my last thoughts will be of him.

Lord Briar grunts, and his hold loosens slightly. I gulp down air at the small reprieve it gives me, but before I can do anything else, the draining begins again.

I am resigned now. This is my consequence. I took too much, now I will have it taken from me.

Suddenly, there is a large crash from behind me, and Fae scream as they fly forward past me and land at Lord Briar's feet.

"You will stop what you are doing to my sister now," I hear Zinn's voice echo from the walls. I crane my head to the side, and I see she is running toward Lord Briar. Wind swirling around her, she is a beacon of light in the sea of darkness. Zinn's hair flies wildly around her, and there is a look in her eyes that terrifies me. They glow with untamed magic. I swing my head back toward Lord Briar and see shock in his eyes. He schools his expression quickly and says,

"Oh, good. Just the person I was looking for. Welcome. Now, I can end you both."

I look back and see Ana and Brone running up behind Zinn, and I allow myself to hope.

"Oh, and two traitors. By the oath I hold over you, kneel," he says, and they both fall to their knees so hard the marble cracks.

BRONE

The floor bites hard into my knees, and I am frozen in place. My sword flies from my hand and skids away into the crowd. Zinn strides forward, power swirling around her. She is beautiful but terrifying. She is the bright spot in the darkness surrounding her. Lord Briar seems not to take notice of the fearsome creature before him, his eyes swirling black pits as he says,

"Let's pick up where we left off."

He raises one of his hands toward Nix and the other toward Zinn.

"You will release my sister, or I will end you," Zinn says, raising her hands.

I struggle trying to rise, but it is of no use. I must bear witness to what unfolds before me, powerless.

Lord Briar resumes draining Nix, and Zinn falters slightly from the pull he sends her way. Then he strikes out, frustrated that it didn't take hold of her, and he shoots vines at her arms. Zinn quickly burns them away with fire so hot it is blue, freeing herself. She turns and rushes to Nix's side. Zinn steps between Lord Briar and Nix, shielding Nix from his attack. Then she throws a torrent of water at Lord Birar, knocking him from his feet. Zinn reaches back with one hand while Lord Briar is down and places it on the stone that is trapping Nix. As soon as her hand makes contact, the stone crumbles to the floor. At the same time, Zinn keeps her water magic flowing from the other hand, aimed at Lord Briar.

"Enough!" Lord Briar bellows and holds his hands up, and the water bounces harmlessly off a shield of ice.

Lord Briar pushes his shield at the water, and the water falls to the floor as harmless snow. My heart sinks. He is too powerful now for her to defeat on her own. Nix reaches for Zinn's leg, and fear fills me. Is Nix going to drain Zinn?

ZINN

I release Nix from the stone holding her captive. Lord Briar's magical hold on her breaks as I shoot a deluge of water at him. Nix reaches up and touches my leg, and I see her. Really see her, and I know what I must do. Lord Briar yells,

"Enough!"

Soft snow falls around us, but I feel no chill. I look at Brone for a heartbeat, turn to Nix and say,

"Let me give you something for once."

I fall to my knees and place my hands on her chest, and give her all that I have. Warmth radiates from where we touch. It spreads through me, and for one instant, we are one. Nothing exists but two little girls staring into each other's eyes in a mirror long ago. I look into her eyes and see all the years I stole everything I took from her, and I replace it with my love. The power in me releases her from all the corruption in her heart. I feel the corruption dissolving, removing its poisonous hold on her heart. I give her my love for the first time: my sister, my other half. The one person that knows me, and I know her. I let my power cover her like an embrace we have never shared, making her whole. As the last bit of my power leaves me, I am weightless for a moment. I look at her kyanite eyes one last time and close mine forever.

ANA

Zinn kneels next to Nix, her hands placed on her chest, and Briar is still. The room is silent as we all watch power swirl between the sisters. An iridescent light emanates from Zinn as she lets her power flow into Nix. Nix gasps and closes her eyes. Peace washes over her features, and the snow flurries freeze in mid-air. The room is silently watching a kind of magic they have never seen before. Beautiful light surrounds the sisters, then recedes to a pinpoint in Nix's chest above her heart. Suddenly, a sonic boom blasts through the room. Everyone is knocked to the floor by the blast. The Great Tree groans, the marble floor cracks, and vines creep up through the floor.

Fae are screaming, some are running from the ballroom. I push myself off the floor. My ears are ringing, and I realize I am free. I am no longer bound to Briar, but how? I look to Brone, and he has dashed into the chaos of the room. I glance at the throne and see that Briar is stunned and knocked to the ground for the moment. I run to Nix and Zinn. Nix is holding Zinn's head in her lap, a tear rolling down her cheek. As I reach them, I realize Zinn is gone. Brone reaches my side with his sword in hand, kneels, and looks at Zinn. He gently kisses her forehead and says,

"I would always follow you."

NIX

I lay Zinn gently on the floor and rise. I am whole. I am free. Brone and Ana stand behind me, free from what kept them bound to Briar. I approach the throne where Briar is stumbling to get his footing. Brone strides past me, and I catch his shoulder. He looks back, and I say,

"He is mine."

Briar flings a hand up, and vines come at me. I bat my hand to the side, and they fall limp to the ground. His eyes widen, and I smile. He then holds both hands up, and I feel a tickling sensation. I realize he is trying to drain me, but it isn't working.

"What magic is this?" Briar says, straining to pull Spirit from me, his face contorting in a mask of rage.

Suddenly, it clicks. The curse is broken. Zinn's gift set us all free, and I know exactly how to defeat the vile being before me.

"I think you know," I say, my voice solemn.

"But how?" Briar says, backing up a flicker of fear passing through his eyes.

"Love," is my only reply.

"That is not possible, you hate her, and she hates you," he stammers and tries to drain me once more.

"No, she never hated me. Now let me show you what love can really do," I say calmly.

I rise to meet him this time, and I hold my hands in front of me. I channel the purest love I received from Zinn and aim it at Briar's heart. The magic hits his chest, and he is lifted from the floor. I twist the magic with my mind and use love's guidance to seek out all the corruption in his heart. Every corner of his being is corrupt and devoid of anything good. The love begins to dissolve the corruption within him. The corruption is being banished as I drive my sister's love into his very Spirit. As the love purifies him, he yells,

"No!" His body arches, pain etched on his face. Then he begins to crumble away, turning to dust. I let the magic flow until he is no more than dust on the wind. I watch every speck of him disappear from view and allow myself a deep breath.

The room is abandoned and silent. I turn to look at Ana and Brone and see an elderly Fae with white hair and travel-worn leathers approaching, and I hold out my hands ready to fight.

"I am free to return home," the old Fae says to himself more than to me. "I see she chose the right path," he continues and gives me a curious look.

"Who are you? I have no quarrel with you, but I will defend myself and my friends if I must," I call out to him. I will not lose anyone else today.

"Skylark. But most call me Sky," he replies, and taps his foot gently on the floor.

The ground shifts, the cracks slowly begin to close, taking the now-melted snow and sealing it beneath the floor, and the vines that cover the ballroom retreat, removing all the chaos left by the fight in an instant.

I freeze. Did he say Skylark? The same Fae that brought about the curse to begin with? How is this even possible?

"Skylark, are you the same Fae that is in the history books?" I ask, cautiously.

"Yes, you see, I too was cursed to be forever bound to this Wood and its fate for all time. I will live the long years of my life protecting those in the Wood who need it," he replies, the weight of his age showing only in his kyanite-blue eyes. "I would like to do something for your sister. If you would permit me the honor?" Skylark asks gently.

"What is it you would like to do for my sister?" I ask, my voice cracking on the word sister as it leaves my mouth.

"I would like to erect a tomb for her here to mark the gift she has given us all," he says solemnly.

"Yes, I would like that very much," I reply, holding back tears.

"Then I shall begin," he says and walks reverently over to Zinn's still form. "Thank you, Zinn. I knew you would choose the right path," he whispers.

Then he gently lays her hands on her stomach, takes a star of the wood flower from his pocket, and places it in her hands. He steps back, and I watch him, my breath coming short. He raises his hands in an elegant motion, and the marble beneath Zinn rises, closing around my sister's body. Silent tears stream down my face. Ana comes beside me, takes my hand gently, and I lean into her. Skylark taps his foot and raises his hands toward the sky, and the marble atop the newly formed tomb, a perfect sculpture of my sister, appears.

I drop to the floor and cry. Ana drops down next to me, and Brone steps closer to Zinn's tomb, placing his hand on the base.

"Why? Why would she choose me, Ana?" I ask breathlessly.

"Oh, my sweet Nix. Don't you see? She loved you," Ana says and embraces me.

I fall into her arms and let my emotions roll out of me. How could I be left behind? Now that I have what I want, freedom, I can't take it back. I can't get her back. My chest tightens, and I can't breathe. Zinn, my constant, my one constant. The light to my dark. Her dark to my light. She really is the one who knew how to love—the one who knew me. Grief rips through me. Guilt curls in my stomach, and I scream. Ana holds me tighter, and I don't ever want her to let go. A light touch lands on my shoulder. I turn to see Brone kneeling next to me.

"Here I found this searching for the boy in the human realm, but I think it belongs to you," he says, and reaches into his pocket and pulls out a small bundle of black hair.

I reach out and stroke the strands of Zinn's hair and think back to the first time I saw her. Zinn's face is full of curiosity, and then her memories pour into me: wanting a mom, needing a friend, and finding love. My heart fractures, and I am her, and she is me, and I will always have a part of her in me. I take Brone's large hand and fold it closed again and tell him,

"She would want you to keep it."

"Thank you," is his only reply, and he stands and turns away, tears in his eyes.

Skylark approaches me slowly and says, "I see you may still be in need. I have brought something for you. It will never replace what you have lost, but it can bring back something that was never really gone," and reaches into his pocket and says, "Give me your hand."

I hold out my shaking hand, and he reaches into his pocket, and I can't tell what he has. His closed hand lies over my open palm, and he says, "Three drops to return."

Something small lands in my hand, and I gasp as he pulls his hand away, and I am holding a beautifully cut blue crystal bottle. I clutch it in my hand. I stand quickly and run from the room. Tears flowing freely from my eyes, I run through the hallways. Ana is calling for me to come back, but I don't stop running. I even push myself with the air and reach my chambers and rush to Cadmun's side.

With shaking hands, I pull the stopper out, tilt Cadmun's chin back, and let a single drop fall into his mouth. I hold my breath and blow it out and say,

"Can you hear me?"

Cadmun remains still, but his breath quickens. I drop the vial to the floor and grab his hand in mine and press my lips against his knuckles. His breathing evens back out. Hope leaves me, and I lean my head on his chest and sob.

"Little Flower? Don't cry. Zinn, did she come? Lord Briar… He wants to kill you… Both of you," Cadmun's voice comes out weak but full of fear.

"She made it. Zinn came. Briar is gone," I say, looking into his eyes.

"It worked, I knew you were never really gone, Little Flower," he says and lightly kisses the top of my head.

BRONE

I hold the small lock of hair in my hand, and tears roll down my cheeks for the first time in many years. I take the hair and place it back in my pocket, and clear my throat. I turn back to see Skylark talking to Nix. He pulls something from his own pocket, and she gasps and runs from the room.

"Wait, Nix, come back," Ana calls out.

"Let her go, she has something important to do," Skylark says, placing a hand on Ana's shoulder.

"Come, we must talk," Skylark says, and leads Ana over to where I am standing. "The Wood is shifting. I no longer feel the presence of the beasts in the tunnels, and the ground hums with balance."

"So, Zinn did break the curse," Ana says and turns to look at the statue, and a tear slides from her eye.

"Yes, she did. Now we must maintain the balance, or we may be doomed to repeat past mistakes," Skylark says, in a warning tone.

"What do you mean?" I ask, hoping Zinn's sacrifice will not be for nothing.

"We must close the portal to the human realm that was torn open by Aura and Poe," Skylark says, warning in his tone.

"How would we do that? Who has enough power to do that?" I ask, confused.

"She does," Skylark says, pointing to Nix walking back in with Cadmun leaning on her for support.

NIX

I walk back to the ballroom, supporting Cadmun. I am met by everyone looking at Skylark and me, pointing a finger at me, with a serious look on their faces.

"Oh Cadmun!" Ana says, hands flying to her mouth, then she rushes over to embrace him.

Cadmun grunts and hugs Ana back. I can't help but feel the deepest gratitude for having them after everything I put them through.

"Come, Nix, we must speak," Skylark says, as Ana steps away from Cadmun.

"Could you help Cadmun?" I ask Ana, and she takes my place supporting him.

I slowly approach Skylark, wondering what he could mean.

"You have a choice to make," Skylark says as I reach him, and Brone looks on with a concerned expression.

"What do you mean? What choice?" I ask, getting nervous.

"You have two paths before you. One will lead to the balance of our world, and one that will only serve you," Skylark says, something hardening slightly in his eyes.

I don't understand what he is saying. I stand waiting for him to continue, and his eyes soften once more.

"You can choose to keep your power, or you can give it all to save the human realm," he says, and I feel my body tense.

I feel the power rolling through me. The love encircling my heart from Zinn, and I don't know if I can let that go. I finally feel whole for the first time in my life. I look at the faces of everyone around me, waiting for my answer, and I turn away from them because I don't know if I can choose.

"If I may, let me give you one thing to consider. Love given away freely can always grow back. It never really leaves," Skylark tells me softly, and I look at Cadmun and Ana.

Cadmun steps forward and reaches for me and wraps his arms around me and says,

"No matter what you choose, just know I will be with you," his voice so soft only I can hear.

In that moment, I feel things shift in me, and I know what to do. I leave Cadmun's arms and turn to face Skylark once more.

"I will close the portal," I say with finality.

"Know you will not have any magic left. You will be human completely," Skylark tells me gently.

"I don't want to make the same mistakes of my ancestors," I reply calmly, looking into his face, and he slightly flinches.

I realize my mistake, even if he was the cause of the curse, he was manipulated by false love.

"I am sorry, I didn't mean to place blame on you. I want to make things right," I say, placing a gentle hand on his shoulder.

He looks into my eyes and nods.

"What do I have to do?" I ask, ready to fully restore balance to the Wood.

"You must go to the portal by the town of Bleaker. Once you are there, you must give all your power to the portal. You must give it freely, or it will not work. When the last of your power absorbs into the portal, it will seal forever, restoring the Wood completely," he says, and I understand.

"I will go now. Cadmun, will you come with me? I don't know if I can do this alone," I admit.

"I will. It would be my honor," he replies and takes my hand.

"Once it is done, come to Solace, the haven that I created long ago. You can start anew there," Skylark says with approval in his eyes.

"I don't know the way," I reply softly.

"Don't worry, the charm around your neck does," he says, and I reach up and touch the necklace. "It is decided. Brone, Ana, you are most welcome to come to Solace as well. I can take you there now," Skylark offers.

"Yes, I would like that very much," Ana says, and moves to stand next to him.

"I must decline at the moment," Brone says, "There are things that I must see to. I must ensure that the Fae do not follow the ways that have led to so much corruption," he finishes, then looks to the statue of Zinn and reaches into his pocket.

"I will always be there to support you on your journey," Skylark says to Brone.

Brone nods his thanks. Then looks to me and says,

"Good luck, Nix. I will take my leave and start rounding up the Fae," and walks away toward the antechamber.

"Come, young one, let us go," Skylark says to Ana, and she shoots him a look.

"My name is Ana. Please don't ever call me young one ever again," Ana quips, and I smile.

"Ready?" I ask Cadmun, and he nods.

I place my hand on the fairy charm on the necklace and will us to the portal outside of Bleaker. I look at Cadmun, and he nods to me again, with reassurance in his eyes. I walk forward to the portal, kneel, and place my hands on the thick ring of clover. I reach deep inside of me to the magic given to me and push. The magic reacts instantly, flowing into my hands. A soft glow appears in the ring, and as the magic continues to flow from me, the glow gets brighter and brighter. I don't feel any fear or any doubt that this is the right choice to make. The magic knows what it is doing. I am just the conduit connecting the Wood with love. I feel a rush as the last bit of power leaves my body, and the very earth seems to sigh. The light that has been building blinds me for a minute, and I have to look away. When I turn to look back at the portal, I no longer see the ring of clover. In its place is a circle of beautiful stars-of-the-Wood flowers glowing softly.

I bow my head and cry into my hands. The love didn't leave me, it still circles my heart. I feel Cadmun's arms wrap around me, and I lean into him. He allows me to cry, and he is my silent witness to the grief I feel inside. I look up to him and am ready to begin a new life. My own life. I kiss his lips gently and say,

"Let's go home."

About the Author

Laura White writes dark fantasy inspired by folklore, Fae legends, and the hidden magic that might exist just beyond the edge of the Wood.

She grew up in Texas and now lives in California with her two daughters, who are the center of her world. Laura has a background in philosophy and previously worked as a hairstylist before pursuing her love of storytelling.

A lifelong lover of books, music, and art, she loves creativity in all its forms. Her late husband, an artist, continues to inspire her imagination and the stories she tells.

I hope you enjoyed Nix's and Zinn's journey. Thanks for coming with me. This completes the **Whispers of the Wood Duology**. If you want to help support my journey, consider leaving a review on Amazon or Goodreads.

Facebook: laurawhiteauthor

Instagram: @laurawhiteauthor

Website: laurawhiteauthor.com

Enjoy the music that inspired the story on Spotify: Laura White Author

www.ingramcontent.com/pod-product-compliance
Lightning Source LLC
LaVergne TN
LVHW040222110826
845146LV00004B/1252

9798234047847